WRONG

WRONG

STORIES

Dennis Cooper

GROVE WEIDENFELD
New York

I'm very grateful to Walt Bode, Bruce Boone, Robert Dickerson, Mark Ewert, Amy Gerstler, John Gill, Robert Glück, Richard Haasen, Ziggy Kramer, Chris Lemmerhirt, Mark Lewis, Ian McCulloch, George Miles, Colin Newman, Felice Picano, Peter Schjeldahl and Brooke Alderson, Ira Silverberg, and David Trinidad.

Copyright © 1992 by Dennis Cooper

Published by Grove Weidenfeld
A division of Grove Press, Inc.
841 Broadway
New York, NY 10003-4793

Published in Canada by General Publishing Company, Ltd.

Due to limitations of space, acknowledgments appear on page 165.

"It Was a Very Good Year" by Ervin Drake, copyright © 1961, renewed 1990, by Linda Bet Music Inc. All rights administered by Songwriters Guild.

Library of Congress Cataloging-in-Publication Data

Cooper, Dennis, 1953–
    Wrong : stories / by Dennis Cooper.—1st ed.
    p.   cm.
    ISBN 0-8021-1401-6 (acid-free paper)
    1. Gay men—Fiction. I. Title.
    PS3553.0582W7   1992
    813'.54—dc20   91-29524
                                                CIP

Manufactured in the United States of America

Printed on acid-free paper

Designed by Irving Perkins Associates

First Edition 1992

1   3   5   7   9   10   8   6   4   2

In memory of

John Bernd
Howard Brookner
Christopher Cox
Robert Davis
Tim Dlugos
Tony Greene
Larry Piet

CONTENTS

WRONG

A HERD

WHEN BELLS RANG to signal lunch period was over, sixty or so students strolled toward the locker rooms, boys into one, girls in the other. Four rows of green lockers crowded with young men, shoulder to shoulder, yanking shirts over their heads, crushing them in small wads. These were tossed in dark cubbies, replaced by gray T-shirts emblazoned with crude block letters: SMITH, WOJNAROWICZ, PETERS, etc. They slipped similar shorts up their legs, over jockstraps.

With tennies, socks bunched in one armpit, they rushed out to the basketball court, slipped them on, stood in organized, memorized rows, and swore at or punched one another. The coach jogged from his office, paused some distance away with his legs apart, hands on hips, bit a whistle tight in his teeth and *toot!* The boys stiffened and yelped their last names in alphabetical order from front to back, twelfth to tenth grade, low to high pitch.

The coach clapped his hands as he rattled off "jump-ing jacks," "sit-ups," "leg-lifts," "push-ups" until the boys panted. Their chests stuck to their shirt fronts. Thin lines of sweat flared in the cracks of fat asses. The whistle fired twice and they crowded onto the track for three laps, while the coach wrote in his book by each name, marking how far they'd run since the first whistle blew.

"There's baseball, football," the coach announced to his rabble. "Don't sit around." They divided into groups of two or three and streaked to their particulars.

Two scrawny ones sat crosslegged against the gym wall with paperback novels, their heads lowered. Three others joined them. Coach Wilson watched, scratched his crewcut. "If they want D's, they'll get them."

"I'd have them in for detention," his junior coach snarled. "Fucking twerps."

"Well, my son's the same way. Future flabbies." Coach Wilson laughed, walked toward a slew of boys tossing a football.

"Over here," he shouted, and one kid fired it to him. "Over there, Jawinsky," he yelled and sent it back two feet in front of the diving boy. "Okay," he continued, "let's make something out of this. I don't have to remind you." The boys picked teams, then formed shapes, lines. They crashed into one another for the bulk of the hour.

Five boys snuck to the empty Coke stand near the bleachers, crouched down in its center, and passed a fat joint around. The dark, cool realm of the stand had the privacy of after-school hours. They could relax there and talk. Sometimes a kid would rush up, AWOL from some ballgame, to buy a few joints for his team. Only once or so in a year would a baseball drop in, hit by some slugger, and force them out of their foxhole.

When one of their members vanished from school, snagged by police, as one or two were every year, other students barely noticed. These boys were so vaguely impressed in the general view. They remained stoned, standing or rocking from heels to toes in front of various backdrops. Or they were statues, tilted back on school walls, whispering deals to the passers. They were less than students, more like fixtures off in the corners of eyes.

Jay Levin did most of the stand's heavy dealing. He had blond hair that spilled from a careless zigzag down head-center and fell in split ends that brushed off his shoulders when he walked around. His face was a nondescript, pimply white, ruled by blue bloodshot eyes. His smile starred a gold tooth where his parents couldn't afford perfect capping. He was known around school for his kindness. When poor kids approached him with pockets turned out, he would grin and tilt his head slightly. "It's good stuff," he'd say, more often than not, then slide a free plastic bag of pills from his wallet.

When Frank, the big dumb kid in Jay's gang, didn't show up at school for a week, most kids who noticed at all told the obvious jokes about where he'd passed out. But Jay and his friends plunked their bewildered expressions with hash pipes and tried to locate him. Banned by his parents, they couldn't call, ask. All they could do was smoke dope and imagine. And after a month they agreed that he'd joined the army or something. He became sort of a legend to them.

But when Jay didn't show up at school for a while, his friends couldn't give up on him. He was their leader. They spread the word around campus. None of Jay's buyers had seen him. One industrious group of Jay's best customers made a flyer, stapled it to the phone poles near school. Two more out-of-it types held a séance, or tried to. The details were too complicated. They wound up just playing his favorite records. Even the coaches, most of whom had bought the odd joint off of Jay, cared enough to telephone the police and discovered they'd already searched themselves out.

WHEN A BOY was undressing in his room, after a full day of school, his homework, a meal, and a single smoked joint, he was relaxed. And if he was watched through a window, cut in three parts by the partly closed shades, by a viewer who had nothing special to do, it was very much like that boy was performing a striptease, although he paid no attention to what he was doing, and how, and in what order his clothes hit the carpet, or in what direction he faced. Everything was seen and judged from the window. It was as if when the boy walked behind his desk chair for a second, obscuring his hips, it was done for a reason.

Outside, the man mulled an aesthetic to fit the occasion and fashioned rewards from these limits. He decided the desk lamp was lighting as reasoned as Nestor Almendros's. The bedroom "set" telegraphed what was to follow. The bed was an obvious lead. The clothes in the closet were clues to this naked young fellow. And so on.

The man crouched, leaves stuck to his clothes. There was no watchdog, or it had been stilled in some fashion. It was too late for mother to stroll out and garden, or for father to hose down the driveway. Whatever brothers or sisters this boy might have were tucked away, snoring or bringing their tiny penises and holes to fruition in ways much too simple to worry about. This boy was old enough to *know*. He pulled off his T-shirt. He yanked down his slacks with his underpants in them like cream in cool coffee. Then he sat on the edge of the bed, towed himself to its center. He touched his cock, got it hard. Joining in, the man judged the slightest veer from tradition. When the boy turned his head, sucked the skin on his shoulder, the boy believed it was a beautiful girl's. The man understood what it was—a young person kissing his own skin—and every move or jerk after seemed richer.

If the boy was fucking a girl it was greater to kneel before them in the soft dirt outside. The girl could, via her range of expressions, tell the observer what he should be feeling while watching the boy. The girl lay on her back, on her side. The boy hunched beside her, head to head, head to crotch, and finally rocking on her, letting a few lines of ecstacy seep past his tightly held jaw and fierce eyes. In this way, he was farther away from the man when he was with her. The man saw more of the body but less of the boy.

But if the boy fucked a boy, the observer had peered in a room stocked with treasure. There was a second kid, maybe as handsome or more than the first. The man could imagine himself in both bodies, sharing the wealth. Or he could smash this windowpane, join them, feel more than his share, have it all to himself. This was the best way to see the boy. This was the heaven that only appeared to exist through windows clouded with breath. The man threw his head back, forgot the boy, came.

The boy wiped himself with a stiff towel, tucked it back under the bed. The man let his cum lie, slipped his cock back in his pants. The boy touched the lamp and disappeared. The man had to duck so his shadow, just scarcely there in the street light, wouldn't cross the boy's kingdom and frighten the king. He walked a long while, past the houses he'd looked at before, ones too dark to hold riches. They were darker yet now. At the end of a street lined with cars, his waited, one of hundreds. He drove across town. Nothing mattered but sleep.

THE WOODS WERE dark and cool at all times. They invited people in at their edges. But miles and miles deeper they stretched and congealed. No one went there. Animals retraced their steps for this or that foggy belief. Little else knew or availed itself of that beauty. Someone would stagger in lost, starving or wounded, fall and die then disappear into animals' mouths. Then, one day much later, maybe men would hike in and carry away the white sketch left behind. They would speak angrily, but nothing around them could understand. So they left things as they were.

If there was a God, He would have liked to lift the cities up in the air with a wave of His hand and plunge them into the woods, leave them there a month, then drop them back at their seasides and into their valleys. He liked the idea of that mixture and grew tired of both the cities' sharpness and the woods' sleep. Wake the woods up, calm the cities down. But He couldn't do this, for unknown reasons. He could only pour rain on the buildings, or snow when He was angry. And into the woods He pointed a hunter once in a while, to stick a sharp pin in its side.

He leaned way over and looked at the town where Bruce lived. A white car was taking uninteresting young men inside it, then driving them to a tract house that

God had to mark with an X to remember. The man who drove the car was as happy as humans could be. Deep in the house, he turned boys over and over like things on a fire. And examined them. And opened them up. The man was learning real secrets and he was growing too powerful. God was jealous. Stripping a boy, killing him would not give God much pleasure. Humans were small. God would have to look through a spyglass until His arm ached.

God wanted to cover this city with ice but thought better of it. Slow down, He told Himself. God lifted the roof off the man's house while he was busy over his victim. There was the man rummaging through a drawer full of tiny sharp objects. God barely understood them. There was the boy covered with blood. There they were together making love. God lowered the roof in its niche. He leaned back until the house, then its city became a small dot on the earth. Less than a dot. The earth was a dot, the most interesting one of the planets. God was flying backward through space, arms and legs stretched out before him like streamers. He looked a little like Martin Balsam when he flailed down the staircase in *Psycho*. But God was laughing, not shrieking. And that was how He would stay.

RAY SEXTON STAYED in bed all day, then into the evening. He handled a newspaper slowly, reading everything scary. Occasionally, he shoved his hand in a bag of Doritos and brought back a dull yellow flower of them for his mouth. Tiny burned chips slipped in unnoticed. His nose squinched up at those handfuls, but he swallowed all down.

The bedroom's decor was phony plush, like the rest of

the house, with an assortment of prints, knickknacks, and furniture that appeared less expensive than they really were. The dresser drawers, picture frames, and tables were pieces of plumed, baroquely cut oak, branded a greenish-gray color, which made everything in his house appear to have a five o'clock shadow.

It was 10:00 and Ray hadn't eaten a full meal since lunch, so he walked to the kitchen. He picked the thick mudlike goop in a plastic jar from the freezer. He licked a chunk off the serving spoon, let it melt on his tongue, drift down his throat, and off into blubber. He thought about boys, those he'd seen today thumbing beachward with T-shirts torn off at their ribs, as was a popular fashion. Too bad they'd been ugly.

Available boys were the dregs. He had to look hard at them for a smart pair of eyes or a sexy mouth. He'd gaze through the acne like a Peeping Tom would through thick bushes. When he had his way, he imagined them as the kids in the teen magazines he picked up at the market. Those magazine's stars were Ray's angels, freed from the limits of IQ's and coordination, whose distant looks had a cloudy, Quaalude effect. Teen stars' perfection haunted him, and a vague resemblance to one or another could, more often than not, be gleaned from the face of a boy he had killed.

A boy chained up or tied down, in the midst of whatever torture, might turn his head sideways and an idol's look would appear in one feature or another. When Ray was lucky it showed across a whole face, as if by magic, as though pulled out of a hat. More often, he wouldn't see the resemblance until the boy died. Then, with facial expressions dulled and in place, Ray would gradually find that the kid brought to mind some ripe child whose

hit songs were stuck on the radio, whose visage beamed
down from most billboards. Then what Ray had done
took on meaning.

Ray scraped out the last of the ice cream, executed a
perfect lay-up of the carton into the sink. "Like that last
boy," he remembered, "so easy to bring down." He had
grabbed a young boy from behind, plunged a full hypodermic right into his arm.

Down in the basement, the unconscious kid had been
strapped hand and foot on a table. When the body was
naked, Ray swept the long hair from its face and no
perfect being emerged. Although Ray squinted, imagined, no angel would fit on the cheekbones or lounge in
the eyes. So Ray brought out the full-headed mask, gathered the hair into a wad at the top of the head so the
piece would fit snugly. He zipped it tight up the back. He
unzipped the eye holes, liked the lids, thought what he
recalled of their contents was pleasant. He unzipped the
mouth hole. He thought the lips were kissable on their
own.

The body was white and smooth. The mask, which
came to a halt at the Adam's apple, was black and rough
like the head of a boy who, suicidal as he'd ever grown,
had stuck his head in a campfire and accidentally lived
on sans hair, ears, his features a hardened blur. Ray's
hands worried over the body from shoulders to feet. The
mask was a fog focused down on the trouble spot, as
black as a spotlight was bright. He massaged the boy's
flesh, but the interior stayed shapeless, the sprawl undis-
turbed, the cock soft. Ray's mouth joined in and a tenderness started to temper his actions. It rose out of nowhere.
Ray loved being close to an almost dead body, smelling
its haplessness, utilizing it as a lover. Then, when he

memorized this surface and needed to know how it curved so and what it could say, he'd want to destroy it and he would say loudly enough so that someone, if nearby, could hear, "No one else will have this opportunity."

Ray's breaths were quick, wordy. The boy's were spaced out and hollow. Ray had his arms underneath the body, embracing the boy, full of ludicrous praise. He crawled on top, sprung his cock from its slacks and rubbed it over the sunken belly. His tongue traced the shoulders' supports. He rested his cheek in a wet spot he'd made.

He looked in the eye holes, at purplish lids. He gazed at the mouth. It seemed as tender as one of his idols', and just the same shape. Ray lifted the head bundle up, lowered his own. He kissed, licked, and shoved his tongue down inside for a while, then withdrew. All that motion had left the lips parted, teeth slightly ajar. And there, flawing the view, lodged inside, was a gold tooth.

"Shit!" Ray whispered, and zipped the slot tight.

Ray stretched on the bed. He felt calm, for once, and would slip into sleep. One hand lay on the pillow, squeezing it gently. He fantasized about the backs of boys' necks where the haircut stopped short and a trace of it trailed just a bit down the skin. He'd place his hand there, fingers behind the ears, scrunching the flesh like a man does a dog's, to relax it. Its mouth would drop open, tongue plopping over its edge. A boy's lips would moisten, swing around as though guided by radar, leak their tongue and its sweets.

JAY LAY ON his back. The lights were on in the room. It was 11:30 P.M. He was asleep again. He had woken up, seen as much as he wanted of real life, and dropped off. Now it was 2:00 A.M. and he was imbedded again, deeper than ever. The same man wandered the room all night, unnoticed by the young man, like the slightest breeze. Jay had sensed busy hands, the smear of a mouth, one short insistent cock.

Jay fell on his back. He raised his head, looked toward a noise. A man was divvying through a large wooden chest, searching for something. The boy couldn't raise farther. Why? He lifted one limp arm toward the man. The man turned, plunged in a needle. The boy's hand dropped and he was asleep again.

The man sat on the basement stairs. A boy slept on a table across the room. The man was deciding what to do next. He had made so much love to the boy, in such depth and detail that the boy wished to die right now. No, the man wanted him to die. With a boy like this, asleep and all, it was too easy to read thoughts into his head.

The boy had been terrified once and screamed like a soldier with bayonet out, bound hand and foot, positive he could box from its grip. "When I break out of these," he'd glared at the man, "you'll be a dead man." But he couldn't undo them. Then he grew sad, numb. He slept. He kept jerking out of his sleep, feeling something too huge in his ass. He fought a while, made it worse, and conked out.

Ray knew this boy. "Under these circumstances," he'd tell a group of the kid's friends, "Jay would scream until he was ugly, and pass out." He'd say it with such seriousness that the friends would just stare at their hands, scuff their shoes on the ground, and agree. He'd face the girls who had slept with the boy, toss them a few easy questions like "What does he do when you blow him?'' and "How much hair in his ass?'' They'd pipe up the answers and think the man jealous. Then he'd narrow his eyes and ask, "When you hack off his balls with a knife and slap his face to keep him alert, does he scream for God or his mother? Or can you, by that point, understand what he says, the way the drugs slur up his speech?''

Ray had blood on his hands, on his pants where he'd wiped them. What to do with the sleeping thing there on the table. It was well known. It had been translated into Ray's language. It kept hiding from him in its sleep. There, such handiwork, and no one to show it to. So Ray woke the formerly cute protrusion at one end a last time, to make sure it was proud of its new look.

The man surveyed it. He felt like a chef on TV. He folded his arms, stared to where cameras would aim and, farther behind, toward an imaginary crowd of old ladies, their withered faces as moved as possible, taking notes, planning to clone his feast in their homes. He looked down on the earth. It was damaged.

"It's time," he said, "to alter this."

The man dumped the last of a pitcher of ice water on the boy's face. It turned but didn't open. He slapped its sides. He leaned down and screamed in its ears. It twitched and rolled. He shook the curly pate, slapped it again. It opened. It had nothing to say. Ray lay the pitcher on one side under it, so it could look down its body, or give the illusion of doing so.

"Good-bye, kid."

Ray french-kissed the mouth. He picked up an ax. He chopped what was beneath him until no owner could claim it. Then he sat down on the stairs. 3:00 A.M. No boy haunted him. Or could. There was a woe unlike any present on earth, Ray thought. He couldn't stop staring through everything. As if he were a god, or were blind. More blind than a god, though he saw what he'd done.

5:51 A.M. Sun in the windows discoloring the curtains. Ray was tired. He was studying the wallet of someone who didn't exist. It had been owned by a boy who'd once stood with another in front of a drugstore and smiled at the camera. Another time he'd been thirteen years old and was hiking somewhere. Here was a shot of a girl. Its back was signed "love." She must have slept with him. Ray peered into her eyes. She looked angry. Here was the older boy Ray recognized, dressed in his T-shirt and jeans at some rock festival. Ray flipped by, couldn't look at it. Too soon after. Here was a Mobil card. Thirty-three dollars. A quarter for emergencies.

Ray picked up a pair of blue underwear. It had been worn by a boy until it resembled him. Ray would keep this, like a bouquet tossed by a bride, to wander deep in a drawer. It would show up on occasion and haunt him when he was looking for something essential. The jeans, jacket—car keys swiped out of its pocket—wallet, socks, shirt, and Adidas flopped into the fireplace and joined their owner in "nowhere."

DEAD BOYS WERE floating up in the headlines, and now those were fading away under heels and in piles out of sight. Most were from Orville Wright High School, where Jay Levin had gone. Its students and teachers were dragging around with their eyes dimmed as artists' erasers. The principal realized this had to stop. So he had someone in his office mimeograph an announcement and deliver one to each homeroom. Teachers, scanning the page just handed them, shrugged and turned to their classes.

"The principal has declared that the final five minutes of first period today will be spent in a reflective silence, in memory of the deceased boys."

Students nodded or stared into space. When the clock touched 8:55 A.M., rows of shushed children pressed their heads down to a stack of their school books as though they'd been whispering something. They thought about records they owned, or beautiful friends. Or they conjured a shadowy herd of the victims. They closed their eyes, let themselves grow very somber, nearly asleep, until the bell rang, then scurried off to fresh classes.

Two coaches sat in an office. The second-period gym students dragged themselves out of their bright clothes, into their grays. One coach spoke to the other.

"Jim, where's that Durand kid, the one you've been training? Haven't seen him much lately."

"He's missing."

"Worried?" Coach Baxter asked.

"To be honest with you"—Coach Wilson quit tying his shoe—"what with all these boys turning up dead . . ."

"Mm." Coach Baxter straightened some things on his desk. Clipboard, keys. "Durand's a tough kid, Jim."

"Yeah, yeah."

"I'm sure he's okay." Coach Baxter eyed the clock, rose from his seat. "Anyway, time to do it."

"Yeah, one second."

"Mm." Coach Baxter shrugged and jogged out.

Coach Wilson laced his sneakers, picked up his clipboard. On the field, Baxter's boys were already doing their sit-ups. His own boys just stood around talking. But seeing their leader, they formed three lines, poised for commands. Thirty attentive young faces.

What the coach dreamed of saying to them—well, three or four of them—didn't matter, especially now. His next words were programmed, all-purpose, expected. *Toot!* "Gentlemen," he said, "run in place," and they did.

JAY HADN'T SHOWN in three days. His parents waited for two, then phoned his friends and police. Nothing. They went to visit the Pearsons, whose son had been missing a year, and whom the Levins had met through the drug busts their loser sons shared. They got together most evenings, sitting in loose circles, arms all over one another. They whispered long repetitive prayers so full of Jay's and Frank's names that an English teacher would have grabbed her blue pencil and changed most to "him" and "that guy."

The last of Jay's gang met in the Coke stand after sixth period on the fifth day. They moped in from the corners of school, threw their books hard against the wooden counters, squatted, and looked imploringly from one to another. They weren't leaders. Bruce knew a lot about movies. Maybe he could say something with meaning in it. Tim's carefulness had always impressed them. They might follow him deeper into themselves and survive. Miguel drove the gang everywhere. Maybe he should do something, swerve this crew back on the track.

They passed joint after joint. No one held up at a certain point so as to stay at least semialert, guide their ranks. None of them knew how. Each hoped another would come up with powers no one had pegged him for.

They smoked and stared. Then, when the dope was gone and the sun fell so low that the shadows they sat in chilled icy, they looked at one another, knees bunched to their chests, teeth chattering, and, like even dumb animals would, stood up and left.

The boys and girls carrying bats, balls up the sidewalk, approaching the school's generous playground, saw the three boys who were having such trouble just crossing the field.

"Look at those guys," one girl sneered.

"Fucking losers."

"Can you see them alive in ten years?"

"No way."

Now the two groups crossed paths on the sidewalk. The gang's eyes had a cataract glaze and stared at unfixed points in the distance. The sporty kids glanced back, saw nothing out there. They didn't know *what* these fucking zombies were after.

"Those guys should just open their eyes," one girl yelled at her steady boyfriend, from her position in left field to his at third base. "This isn't bad." She indicated the field, themselves, the stores around school. Then she punched her glove, bellowing to a boy at home plate, "Hit it here, Jackson!" The kid at bat bowed, firmed his grip, and struck out.

In the car, Miguel turned to his friends. "Where to?"

"Any ideas?" Bruce asked Tim.

"Not really. I guess we could go look for Jay, but I wouldn't know where."

"I'll put on some music," suggested Miguel. He pushed in a tape of The Who.

It was dialed loud. They could feel its bass line rumbling in their jaws. They slouched in corners of the car, rested their heads back, and crooked their left arms as if fingering frets on guitar necks. Their right hands held invisible picks between thumb and forefinger, slashing the air just in front of their belts. If they weren't crazy, they were a band. If they were a band, they were one that had lounged its career in rehearsal, down a long stretch of highway, on poorly lit stages, repeating the songs of the stars. But they grew content in that way and, after ten songs, when their hair matted in sweat and arms cramped, Miguel drove the sleepy bunch off. It didn't matter where. They just cruised for a while.

It was late night. One by one they were home. Each boy's parents heard him stagger in and glanced at the clock. 2:00 A.M. on a school night. Where had he been? But when they got up to ask, he'd just get sullen or violent. So, if they loved their son, which they probably did, they left him alone. Lying there, ears on his crashing around, they hoped that sleep, if anything left on the earth, might settle him down and rearrange this wild disarray, like some flowers, for them.

AT 2:00 A.M. the phone rang in the Levins' house. Mr. Levin lifted his head from the pillow. His wife slept soundly. He reached over her, snagged the phone on its third ring.

He tried to say "Hello." It sounded more like a croak. He cleared his throat and said, "Yes?"

"Is this the Levin residence? Mr. Thomas Levin?"

"Right."

"I'm sorry to disturb you. This is Lieutenant Peterson of the West Los Angeles Police Department. We've found a body that matches the general description of

your son. Could you possibly come down here this morning and check?''

Mr. Levin blinked at the clock. "Uh, I'll be there.
You're on Federal, right?''

''Yes. Thank you, Mr. Levin. Very sorry to disturb
you. Good night.''

His wife had lifted her head at one point but was
sleeping again. "Jane?'' He shook her shoulder. "Jane.''
She opened her eyes and he told her.

They crowded into the bathroom, applying cold water
to shiny faces, bringing their haircuts to life in his comb
and her brush. They were in their late forties but looked
much older these days. Jay, their son, had been wasted
the last several years, since he'd found drugs in eighth
grade. His nature was still very sweet, but it was so
ragged, a wilderness. The yard games that he and his
father once couldn't stop playing were lost on him now.
Long walks he'd shared with his mother were planted
like interviews there in the house: "Where have you
been?'' "Around.'' "What are you thinking?'' "Nothing.'' He'd gotten too stoned or whatever to answer.

Mr. Levin pulled on yesterday's suit. Mrs. Levin
slipped on a loose dress. It wasn't until they were in the
car that they felt what they had to.

''I just pray to God it's not Jay,'' she sighed, and folded
her hands, pressed them against her chin.

He wanted to say that it wouldn't be, but it could be.
No one knew yet. Not the police who stood over a body
and bantered the Levins' good name. Not he, a man at
the wheel, too tired to think about dying, or let it deter
him. They drove in near silence the rest of the way. At
stoplights he'd hold her hand, gaze at her. She would
stare at his eyes. "I know,'' he'd say softly. But he
didn't.

"Mr. Levin?" A policeman walked up from behind. They'd paused at the main desk, looking around for directions.

"Yes, sir."

"This way."

Mr. Levin's arm crossed his wife's shoulders. Her arm surrounded his waist. Their limbs had moved there at some point on the drive. He noticed and glanced at her. She glanced back. To him, she seemed terrified. To her, he looked amazed. The policeman opened a door, following them in.

"The Levins?" asked a man at a desk.

"Yes," they and the officer answered together.

"This way."

The four approached what was clearly a body disguised by a blue sheet. Mr. Levin tightened his hold on his wife to protect her from it. He wondered what he felt. Nothing or numbness. The feeling was vague like the form they approached. The blue looked like water. Like a combination of cloth and water. Wet cloth. Now they stood above it. Blue cloth and the soft curves of a body.

"The tooth that's supposed to be gold is missing. Other than that it matches the description we have." The fourth man was speaking. Who was he? He lifted the sheet at one end, then back, not without a feel for dramatics.

"No," Mr. Levin said. It was a boy with long hair like Jay's, a big nose like Jay's, maybe Jay's chin. But it was not Jay. "No, it's not him."

"Okay," the man said. He looked weary. This would mean more work for him. The boy was covered again. "He must be a runaway, then. I'm sorry to have brought you here. Good night." He pushed the body and table away, toward a dark part of the room.

"I'll lead you back," the policeman offered.

As they went, Mr. Levin asked questions. It relaxed them a little. ". . . and we'll call you when we find anything further." Mr. Levin liked the officer or, rather, how steady he was, speaking the lines with a firmness that he could admire even now.

In the car, Mr. Levin exhaled loudly, in relief. "Well, it wasn't Jay," he stated, just to say something.

"But the boy it was, the poor empty thing . . . so silent . . . more like a ghost than a young man, really. If it had been Jay in that condition this would have been hell."

"The officer said that the boy overdosed on drugs. They found him in an abandoned house . . ."

". . . like a ghost . . ."

". . . naked like that. They couldn't find clothes anywhere. But there were no signs of molestation." He paused. "He looked somewhat like Jay."

"But skinnier and his face looked crazy, not like Jay's at all."

He fit one arm around her. "Jane, it wasn't Jay. We should feel good about that." She was acting indulgent. He worried she'd drink soon as they arrived home. She'd wind up crying. "Let's go right to sleep when we get back. Sleep will wipe this away."

"I hope so."

He squeezed her, then brought both hands back to the wheel. In the silence that followed they thought about Jay. Mr. Levin pictured a boy around twelve years of age, ten feet away, with his hands out, awaiting a ball. Mr. Levin threw it. Jay caught it and grinned. They didn't have to say they adored each other. The game had implied it. That ball flew back and forth as if tied with a note. It read "I love you," meant freshly each toss.

Now Mr. Levin saw Jay in his bedroom—the Jay who had disappeared. The boy looked tired. That genuine smile was still there, but it grew too easily, stayed too long. He had told his son to turn in, it was late; Jay had looked back intensely, as if at a text. An ashtray of stubbed joints between the boy's knees explained why.

"Jay," he'd said, "turn in." And, getting no response, he'd said it again, almost inaudibly and very tenderly, feeling so strange in the hold of that gaze.

"Turn in."

Mrs. Levin pictured Jay dead on a table, covered by a sheet in a city far away. People like her and Mr. Levin looked at his face, said "No," and drove home. He'd look so light he could be blown on the floor with a sigh. He'd look so cold she would cover him with a blanket, then her coat. She'd wrap her arms around her shivering self and pore over him. His face was going to turn brown and flake from its bones like a sunburn, somewhere in the future when she had forgotten it. A skull would cut through, growing whiter and whiter until it was more like a light than the boy she'd known. "Jay," she said softly.

As they drove everything grew unbelievably bright.

THE THEATER LIGHTS were so dimmed that Bruce had to linger by one of its doors for several minutes until a sunnier outdoor image onscreen focused rows of seats from the darkness. He slid into one near the back and hung his legs over the chair in front of him.

Up there, a chauffeur was driving a fairly attractive brunette down a highway. She looked worried.

"Jeeves?" She leaned forward, close to his ear. "I said

I wanted to go to my friend's house. This isn't the way."

"Relax," he growled, swiveling his head.

As usual, at least in the porno Bruce had seen, the man wasn't nearly as cute as the woman. Now he parked the car, turned to her.

"You and I can have more fun than you and your girlfriend."

"Ooh," she purred, "I'd been hoping you'd ask."

What unbelievable and sexist shit, Bruce thought.

The man helped himself into the backseat, undressed her and himself. They had sex in the usual ways, with the typical breathy rewards. Bruce was bored, but he had an erection and waited for it to relax so he could go home.

Lying in bed late that night, his tired eyes on a newscast, he remembered the sex he'd seen. Finally, exhausted, he could safely know sex as the powerful gesture it was. He remembered the actress, the actor made plain so that men in the dark could project themselves over him, like holograms onto an animatron. Then Bruce was masturbating. The naked girl was a springboard. He imagined kissing Jay. He stripped his friend's body. He plugged his hard-on in Jay's smile, then ass. A smooth palm played their parts.

Bruce came. When he opened his eyes, he was alone. Jay had swung down like a pendulum out of the indistinct ceiling, then flew out of sight the very second Bruce wanted.

Ray Sexton saw what he could through a window. He knelt on damp, saucy ground, among cold ferns and drainage pipes. A slit in the curtain framed the room's light, Bruce's role in it. Ray stayed in his spot until the scene was switched off.

In the dark, Bruce pulled his pillow close, like it was
Jay. They rocked. Instinct told him to go find his best
friend wherever he was. But Bruce was afraid that by
morning he'd feel as removed as he did before lust had
invaded. He knew that the language of lovers was simple, like that of the primates. All words pointed in and
meant joining in one sense or another. That wasn't for
him.

He unwrapped himself from the pillow, fit it under his
head. It would be nice, he admitted, if this were Jay's
stomach or thigh and the black blur the world became
this late at night could, like a white wall, be projected
with elsewhere when he grew too bored. Then he turned
his back on the room.

Walking gradually down the sidewalk to his car, when
the chum of his hard-on had fled, Ray would think of
himself as a scared man, as what he was. Watching the
boy just now, he hadn't wanted to lie beside him and
stutter how much he loved hairless bodies, though that's
how he felt. Instead, he wanted to screw the boy's ass
with whatever he could keep hold of, until that body's
one rest stop matched its frantic compadre, the face.

On nights like this, when he wished a boy into his
grave but that boy still breathed and the dream-corpse
popped like a bubble, Ray felt deeply apart and away.
He'd come, but wished he could draw the sperm back in
his body, go kill a boy and let it loose there. Things
didn't feel sexy, and when Ray wasn't horny or couldn't
be, he was worthless. He thought about suicide. He was
afraid there was another lifetime just after this one,
where boys he'd killed had ganged up. They lingered for
him in the darkest mood between the decision to live or
to die. He wasn't sure what they could do to him once

he was dead, but it would be monstrous.

Where was Ray's car? He'd walked blocks past it and turned with a shrug, headed back. "I'll live," he knew, with the same shrug.

It was a warm night. Bruce sweated in his sleep, even with the windows open a bit and a lone sheet crumpled down at his knees. He lay on his stomach, one leg crooked to the right, his ass open a crack, its stink overcast there like the least of bad breaths, someone's last.

In a different world Jay would lean down, hold his tongue until Bruce's every taste, texture, odor were his to recall. Bruce would sleep or pretend, wishing love was this easy, implied by such sweetness of thought, more like a wisp of religion one could simply inhale from another boy's skin without breathing a word.

The man in the porn film would twist one soft edge of his mustache, leer at the infrared camera, and silently smack his lips at such buttocks. He would reach down, slip one hand under each hipbone, and lift Bruce's ass like the lid off of something, sniff to make sure it was clean, then worm in his tongue.

Ray would cover this face with a rag soaked in chemicals, send the boy deeper than ever. He might treat this ass gently at first, so that he'd like it and so that he'd know what he ruled. Then he'd try to tear it in half like a telephone book, or center it in the sight of a shotgun. Awash in Ray's slopping of kerosene, Bruce would chill, start to wake up. Ray would step back. A lit match would Tinkerbelle down.

JAY LEVIN DASHED from the Coke stand to locker room later than even his lazy friends had. By the time he'd snuck to his slot in the green metal rows, only a few of the stragglers lingered behind, tying the last of their shoes. He'd be late for his next class, no matter how quickly he changed, so he relaxed, let it go.

He peeled off his stinking gray T-shirt, kicked his Adidas and a tangle of jockstrap toward his compartment. The shower room was a white tiled chapel running along the right side of the lockers. Ten or so nozzles aimed down from each of five sparkling columns. He'd never done more than peer into that realm with amazement before, at the white bodies and steam that enhanced them. Now he stepped to a nozzle, grabbed its handles, twisted them, and let out a yelp as the water practically inhaled him, back first.

"Fuck everything," he sighed aloud, as his long blond hair darkened and snaked down into his eyes.

Outside, it had started to rain. Jay stood in the entrance awhile, hoping it would ease up. A jock in a T-shirt and shorts strolled up the walkway, not even trying to cover his head. Looking at him, Jay felt cold. And the jock, seeing the boy was unfriendly, wandered by mumbling incomprehensible threats. Finally, Jay ran up the direction the jock had come, into the parking lot. It was too late to go to his class, so he drove into Hollywood, hoping to unload a few wads of his just-purchased kilo. Just fuck the whole rest of the day.

A bunch of boys were standing around on the sidewalks over a several-mile stretch of Hollywood's dumpiest boulevard, in front of its bars and taco stands, selling the bulge in their pockets. Some had their thumbs out halfheartedly so police couldn't snag them for loitering. Some just stood on the corners and scanned through slow-moving cars. If young guys were driving, the scan was a leer. If an officer, or an old person, or family, the scan was indifferent. Those cars weren't going where boys were. Customers wandered the sidewalks, and dealers hissed out the luscious words "grass" or "hashish" to each passer. Some kids would stop, exchange greens, then follow the sellers to nearby parked cars.

Ray had searched everywhere for a victim that evening—chic Westwood, outside nightclubs, in pinball parlors. It was well after midnight. All respectable children were off in their beds. He'd have to wipe a kid off the boulevard. Boys there were easy. Because they were druggies, the worst was expected, so when cops found them dead they just heaved them straight into the ground. Ray had picked his earliest victims from its ranks, before he'd discovered the high school's.

Ray was cruising it now. In the low light of street lamps and neon bar logos, the long-haired boys glowed at first glance, like the young courtiers in Renaissance paintings that Ray had kissed as a child. By the third or fourth go-round, bright doorways and closer checks revealed age marks, scars, and flaws in conception. A shimmering reef of red hair covered the mug of a pirate. What seemed a doll's face was hit by a headlight and looked like the man in the moon's. It was more than an hour before he saw one that he could imagine was decent. Even so, this face would gradually end up in the mask.

Ray's car, which had been rubbing the curb where Jay stood, came to a stop. He climbed out and approached, made an offer, then followed the boy to a car parked on a side street, between two lampposts, under a tree that would keep their transaction a secret. It made Ray's hypodermic seem like a magician's or doctor's swept out

of his pocket and plunged into Jay's upper arm with an
unnoticed flourish.

Hours later, at 4:00 A.M., when it had been dark long
enough to bore nearly everyone on the earth to sleep,
Ray carried a heavy, dusty bundle out of the basement up
to the garage. He tossed it on the backseat of an auto. It
was a carpet rolled around something. A boy's shaved
head was just visible inside one end like the fruit of a
Chapstick.

He drove the San Diego Freeway beyond the Sepul-
veda Pass into the suburbs. The offramp at Ventura Boulevard was empty and, on its left side, bracing the hill
back up to the freeway, thick trees suggested a wilderness. But the illusion halted abruptly behind them, at a
rocky gray slope. When Ray parked the car, clawed
through the foliage, and found a spot for his refuse, he
was surprised to learn that the earth still felt warm. Like
skin, he realized, just after death when there was no hint
of the sentence passed over it.

Ray sprawled out in the mixture of moonlight—far
left—and the sun—far right—catching his breath at one
end of the carpet. The boy perched on the other, as cold
as a sculpture that Ray had stolen from some art museum
and broken. It was worthless to him and to them. All he
could do was dump it somewhere. With a kick of his shoe
it slid down the dirt, lodged in the fleece of damp grass
below.

Wallowing back through the bushes, Ray thought
how the corpse might stay permanently hidden, a distant white blur to the hurrying drivers, like their expressions in choppy pond water. It was a sight that
would smear in the mind, be erased by the long straight
freeway, grow vague as the date, as the night would

become, then the month and everything not photo-
graphed in it.

Dear Mother,

I'm dead. That was me in the abandoned house. I fooled
them. You can sleep now. I don't think I miss you, but
I thank you for all that you've . . .

The paper flew out of her hands. It twisted and skidded across an empty parking lot. She couldn't chase it
fast enough. When she tripped and fell she found Jay
prone beneath her. He looked like the boy she'd seen on
the table.

"He's still alive," she realized, and got to her feet. She
ran toward a warehouse. Its door was open, her husband
inside. She threw a glance over her shoulder. Jay had
stood up. She turned and ran at him. Halfway there, she
woke up.

It was morning. Mr. Levin was showering. She was
covered with sweat.

"Jay's alive," she whispered. Then she felt crazed for
believing her dream. "God help me," she sighed. And He
did.

A car had broken down on a freeway. Its driver and
passenger stood around, waiting for someone to help
them. The sun made everything sparkle. In its midst, the
taller one narrowed his eyes. He was looking over the
edge, toward an offramp. There was something down in
the bushes. They agreed, then skidded down on their
shoes and their hands.

It was Jay.

Bruce sat behind Tim; Miguel steered. They kept their

sights over the five cars ahead, on the black one. Jay was
inside it. They'd blathered about his death for three
days. Sadness had passed mouth to mouth, like mono. It
showed in their car, which was usually swerving, now
practically towed.

The Levins followed the hearse. This time the body
they'd checked on was theirs, and it hadn't been cool and
collected like the other boy's. Murder had changed it.
They had to gawk at their son just to see him. First he'd
been molested. Then he'd been chopped up and dropped
by a freeway. That's all they knew or wanted to know.

Mr. Levin was angry, strangling the wheel. Mrs. Levin
was calmer. She wished they were burying her boy, not
that creature who once had been Jay. What situated itself
in that black car scared her. When she imagined, as she
did, the lid of the coffin raising up, something crawled
out and attacked her. If that ruined Jay was to rise from
its box and try to get home she would ask her husband
to pull his gun from the bedside table and shoot it.

"Into the ground, that's where a coffin fits. It doesn't
belong out here. The earth's sharks," thought Bruce,
surveying the graveyard, each flat white stone like a
buoy warning of who was below. He scanned the hundreds of students in a dense ring around Jay and his
parents. Bruce had passed most of them in the hallways
at school. But in these black suits, with their loud
mouths shut down and eyes lowered, they seemed to be
actors who'd played those wilder roles.

The priest stopped intoning and waved his hand at
Jay's father. Miguel squinted. The man looked like Jay
probably would have if he'd made it into his forties.

Mr. Levin unfolded a few sheets of paper. "I want to
read something," he said, "which is the lyric to a song

Jay and I used to listen to when he was a boy. It was a favorite song of mine. I didn't think he understood what it meant, but not long ago he heard me playing it and told me it said a great deal about my feelings for him and, indirectly, his for me."

He looked at the young mourning faces. For a moment he thought he might have made a mistake. This was an old song. Maybe these youngsters would laugh. But their faces looked up at his, he decided, with curiosity and respect.

"When I was seventeen, it was a very good year. It was a very good year for . . ."

"Oh God," Tim thought, hearing the words. How typical of Mr. Levin to pick a song Jay didn't care about. When someone's a child he listens to whatever's out in the air. So maybe Jay recognized this piece of shit and said something nice to his father. Tim didn't expect to hear Hendrix or Townsend, but these words were so far away. Jay would never be senile enough to express them.

"When I was twenty-one, it was a very good year. It was a very good year for small-town girls who lived up the stairs, with perfumed hair that came undone, when I was twenty-one."

Bruce stood next to Tim. The fact of the song's inappropriateness hadn't occurred to him. He thought of how powerful the lyrics were, in their archaic way. He could almost imagine an orchestra in the background, Jay standing there, singing these words in a cloud of dry ice. Bruce tried to hone in on the shape of Jay's body, nude, as glimpsed in gym classes. He knew what he'd felt for that body, though he was too stoned to say now for sure.

Mr. Levin stopped reading and took one step back, instinctively, army-fashion. The priest unfolded his hands, began to speak about what Jay had meant. His voice was a rosy old drone that sent each mourner off into his or her daydreams. Eventually the sermon was less than a negligible backbeat herding them on. He lowered his voice, said, "Amen," and the funeral ended.

Jay's friends who the Levins approved of edged up to them. Death was vague, no matter how atheist or religious one happened to be, but implicit in it was the thought that embracing friends, enemies, strangers could help, so people hugged for the next several minutes.

Bruce hugged Tim, then Miguel. They looked so loaded to him. Once on mescaline Bruce had decided if he drank an orange juice each morning he'd never feel lonely again. Now he gazed in Tim's bloodshot eyes, Miguel's, and thought if he looked in them every day he'd stay happy.

The Levins shook every hand that was open, then walked to their car, his arm around her, her weight on him. Jay's friends fanned into the evening. Bruce, Tim, and Miguel drove to the Coke stand and plowed themselves under the dope and the darkness.

After the crowd drove away, several workmen with shovels climbed the graveyard's green hill, slightly drunken, like dreams might approach sleeping heads. Jay's coffin was waiting, its painted brown surface as neat as a bedspread, with no indication of what lay inside.

RAY SEXTON SPRAWLED on his bed. He'd been napping most of the day. To his right was the latest headline. Police had found one of his victims. There was a photograph on the front page. "He didn't look like this," Ray said to himself. This one had his hair combed, was wearing a tux. The boy Ray had fucked with was less of a "yes man" and dirtier, drowsier. Poring over the photo, Ray felt like a parent who'd made the mistake of gazing into his son's open coffin. It refocused Ray's vague impression of his victim. This was not what he'd killed.

There was a tenderness inside the body, like there was the corpse of a beautiful boy in the ground. It lay that cold and far away, seen only by the hungriest eyes, the weepiest blue. When Ray thought of someone he needed, he felt empty. When he knew he'd get what he wanted he felt empty. In every cool body something could warm without reason. His hands would veer from his work, anchor him at the flesh. But when it grew cold he felt nothing. Before, he wanted it. Now it felt cold and empty.

Ray looked at the face of the boy in the newspaper. The young man had put his lips close to a camera, pouted. The camera had focused, flashed. The face had slid through a hole in its side, unfogging slowly. The face was reduced, on a page full of landscapes, all their homes burning and inhabitants charred. There was the boy like a hostage among them. Ray wished he could hand this boy his photo to autograph. The boy would write "loved you," then his first name. It was printed below. Jay. It rose from death like a single bone from a tar pit.

Once that bone was a boy. It moved about freely amid some hysterical pinball machines, in cars sliced out of Star Wars. Pimples dotted his face. He hugged girls closer than Ray could imagine. Arrogant scowls arched his eyebrows. He'd argue with girlfriends, get mad, walk home. Ray tore the picture out of the paper. He tacked it to a bulletin board, by the others. Five cute boys whom he'd known. A row of cute tilted heads that wished black and white photos were manholes that they could crawl out of. Five heads hung high by a hunter.

Where Ray stood, there was a smell that he'd sweetened with Lysol and blown around the room with a portable fan. It had stayed, as if a ghost, as though it were lazy. Ray had noticed it two weeks ago in a spot in the hall and one by the sofa. He'd searched their shadows and just come up dusty. Then it had covered the house. He'd put bodies down in the crawl space, like beasts into a cage. Now they reached up and swiped at him through the floor boards.

For days, this odor had quashed his plans. The ideal had grown sour. Then, gradually, the longing came back. This new wrinkle and stink added force to it. It made boys seem even more delicate, midway between childhood and . . . Ray swept his hand through the sickly air. He'd told the most recent boy to breathe deeply. "Know what that is?" he'd mused. "That's where you're going." The boy had looked bewildered. It was a concept almost as vague as a heaven, but, unlike God's campground, a boy could sniff this one and know it was real.

Ray flipped on the TV and stationed himself on the end of his bed. It was a console model, which Ray had acquired, as he had his whole house, with the money left him by his parents. They'd died when he was twenty, in the crash of a light plane. And now on the TV news a reporter was saying a plane had gone down just that morning. It seemed like one fell every day. Ray's loss was one of millions.

The dead boy's face came on screen. It stared several seconds, followed by a crude sketch of another found just a few days before, unidentified still. It didn't do the kid justice. Ray hadn't used the mask over him. The face was ground in his mind like a boot heel. A newscaster was saying police had connected the murders. This was old news. They were looking around for the creature who'd done it.

"Good luck!" Ray exploded in laughter.

If there was a God, He watched this and wallowed. Not that He didn't have head colds to decongest elsewhere and better monsters on earth and in space, but He'd grown obsessed, for imperious reasons. The greed and resentment still perked in His eyes, but His alternate choices were snuffing this interesting scene, which would be fruitless, or slipping some clue to police, and that would be meddling. Better, He knew, to let it go on as it had: incomprehensible, beautiful. God leaned down closer. There was the man in his window, acting just crazy. There were the lonely friends kneeling at edges of bedtimes, with prayers floating up and their faces cast down. What kind of logic was that, He wondered. "Let them be nothing." He watched a while longer, but prayers were the dull part and death the most boring of all. Enough for today. He let Himself drift slowly away like a freighter unloaded of all its cargo, with only His eyes on the man where he'd stopped for one final idea before dreaming.

Ray stood at the bedroom window, dead tired. With the darkness outside and the light on inside, it was a mirror. He'd remembered something deep in his past, a trick with the glass that his mother had taught him when he was much younger. She'd positioned him so, turned every light in the house off except for a candle she held a few inches under his chin. When he'd stared at his face a long time, not blinking, his features had softened and changed, grown scars, other hair, different noses and eyes. She'd said these were his faces in previous lives.

Either she had been crazy or that candle special because there was nothing here now but exhaustion. Daylight would show up and scrub it away on red knees. Ray would see outside again, master boys, make them nothing. But first everything had to grow darker, be covered completely, make him shiver as he shivered now when he turned out the lamp's light and slept.

(1980)

CONTAINER

for Tony Greene

THE SUMMER I graduated from high school my grandparents paid for a short trip to Amsterdam. I'd read about the cafes where, in place of food, waiters held out trays piled with drugs. Police stayed "cool." Hustlers lined the canals, ubiquitous as street lamps. A worldly friend mentioned some "Houses with Boys," businesses stocked with lascivious teenagers. Cover the cost of their next meal or fix and they'd escort you into a private room, strip, lie face down on a bed, glance back over their shoulders, and mutter something like, "Do what you want." I still remember the look on his face when he said that.

I found a hotel near the red light district. It was clean but cramped. At dusk I peeled an orange and headed into the catsupy stain on my city map. I found myself on a

39

narrow street lined with four-story townhouses, each charred with several centuries' dirt. Their windows had been enlarged at some point in the past. Instead of the usual living quarters, each framed a bright pink compartment too petite to be someone's bedroom but larger than, say, a Joseph Cornell box. But where you'd expect a collage there stood a woman or girl wearing tons of makeup, scantily clad, a seen-it-all look on her face.

I watched a man fix his eyes on one cubicle two stories up. Its tenant shook herself out of a daydream, stepped behind the pink backdrop. He pushed a button next to the street level door, was buzzed in. Every few minutes another old guy would follow suit, entering one of the countless doors that lined the street, glancing nervously over his shoulder. I tried the next block. It was identical—rows of display cases with the occasional pink blank. I tried to imagine the scenery behind those vacancies. I saw a woman's closed face, a man's face wrenched open, a puny hard-on, a gigantic vagina.

I found a block packed with porn bookstores, entered one, and started thumbing through magazines. Everything seemed to be legal. Stuff that would've looked slightly ridiculous in the States, like horses fucking men, was just the tip of the iceberg. There was a whole shelf devoted to family orgies, their bodies all different sizes, their faces slight variations on one look. In other rows men plunged fake knives into fake lovers' stomachs at orgasm, young girls licked old women's wobbly ass-cracks, infants with mouseholelike eyes played contentedly in the spray of a moaning man's piss.

After about a half-hour of browsing, the man at the counter yelled, "Make your choice." On a lower shelf I hadn't scanned yet I saw an issue of *Lad* with a skinny brunet on the cover. He had a few pimples in the predictable nooks and a blank, washed-out face into which you could read any mood that you needed. ''This store is not a museum,'' the clerk growled as he taped shut the paper bag. I grabbed my purchase, took a deep breath, and asked for directions to ''Houses with Boys.'' His response was a look so contemptuous I couldn't see anything else for an hour.

Back at the hotel I flopped on the bed. I lit my hash pipe and untaped the bag. There was that kid again—pale face, mouth open, head tilted back like a singer attempting to hit an extremely high note. I added up his quaint genitals, plaintive eyes, AC/DC T-shirt, and made a guess he was thirteen, fourteen. He stripped and posed awkwardly for the first several pages, sat down on an unmade bed, grinned at the camera, glanced up, grinned at a fat, balding man who was sitting down next to him.

The man gripped the boy's head, lowered it to his thighs, as if preparing to hike it. Greasy hairs spewed out between his white knuckles. He licked the boy's nipples like pieces of candy. He held the boy down, fucked his spitty mouth. A wrinkled hand flipped a delicate penis from side to side. The photographs left nothing out, from the soles of the boy's callused feet to the hairs fine as spiderwebs trickling down his nape. But when the man finally got to the asshole, he turned up a kind of gargoyle where he'd surely sought something more rosebudesque.

It was black from the number and size of the things men had shoved in. An inch of the interior stuck out, forming thick wilted lips, droopy and slick like a panting dog's. The man skinned it back so one could see the extent of the damage. Huge as it grew, I was surprised when I turned the page. The man's fist had squeezed inside. Maybe the boy had passed out, because his face had a peacefulness I still don't believe in. Or he was dead, but I couldn't consider that. Anyway, he didn't change his expression for the rest of the sequence.

I can't remember the details of how I felt. Not completely turned on, though I know I jerked off. Being inexperienced, I naturally responded to the chance to explore someone pretty, and, once the model's amazing resemblance to Phillip sank in, I must have felt overwhelmed by the thought that my friend could have wound up like Lad, a mere example of youth at the crux of some stranger's lust. I closed my eyes and imagined my hand inside a teenager's body. I felt out of this world, on top of Lad's world, and Phillip looked like he should look—gone, buried, forgotten, out.

I misplaced that magazine years ago, or someone stole it. When I discovered its absence, I felt like somebody had dug Phillip's body up. He was loose again. He possessed lovers, his smirk on their faces the way a lost child's seems to be on the muzzle of the "tame" tiger he was last spotted petting. Phillip hovers just inside my daydreams, unseen but omnipresent. And once in a while I try to kill him off. I shove the knot of my feelings as deep as they'll go into as compact and smoothed-out a prose style as I can build out of what I know. But they don't belong here, any more than a man's fist belongs in a boy's ass.

(1990)

INTRODUCING
HORROR HOSPITAL

FRANK AND DOUG, two high school students, arrived
stoned and drunk at the Undo Club in North Hollywood.
By day the trendiest clothing and shoe store, at night it
was *the* hippest place to waste time. They squeezed
inside, found an area to stand near the stage.

An overweight girl in shredded clothes sauntered up to
the microphone. "Welcome to the world-ignored Undo!"
she bellowed. "Darby Crash will be on soon, but first
. . . Here they are, from Reseda—Horror Hospital!"

To sparse applause, four scrawny teenagers hooked in
their instruments. One stepped to the microphone, running a hand through his spew of blue hair. He stared
blankly at the audience for a couple of seconds. "Oh,
hi," he yawned. They began their first number.

Frank pulled his super-8 camera out of its case and

plugged one eye, scanning the people to either side of him. They flailed around to a series of roughly hewn songs with names like "Let's Not (And Say We Did)" and "Fuck Dead People." Frank figured maybe he'd intercut this footage later with scenes from *Woodstock* to make a generational comment.

Doug watched the band carefully, hot for its singer, a pasty waif screaming elementary phrases stocked with obscenities. As a rule Doug thought punk rockers were sex gods. He'd always liked the last-legs look.

The band's short set ended abruptly. They walked off. People clapped politely. Frank put his camera away and hit the bathroom. Two minutes later Doug spied the waif sipping a beer at the bar and walked over. "You were terrific," Doug said. "A little," the boy smiled. "What's your name?" Doug asked. "Trevor Machine," the boy answered, "and yours?"

Doug tried not to laugh. Some New Wave pop stars were changing their names, picking ones that were nasty and clever. It had become a new kind of tradition. But "Trevor Machine" sounded stupid. It was the choice of a mental deficient. Doug was charmed. "Doug Wasted," he said facetiously.

DOUG KNOCKED ON Frank's bedroom door and went in. Frank threaded a short reel of film into his projector and motioned for Doug to sit down on the bed. He flicked off the room light, centering a square gray beam on the uncluttered wall. Once focused, it was the crowd at the Undo last weekend.

Doug sat forward admiring the view and Frank's technical savvy within its dim limits. "Brilliant framing," he said. Still, he wondered when Horror Hospital would take their rightful place.

After a gradual pan to the left, they appeared. Doug hadn't thought about Trevor, outside of a few jerk-off fantasies, since that night. Robbed of the deafening soundtrack, reduced to a kind of mime, Trevor's presence seemed far less unique than it had.

The mock-angel of doom was a boy who'd spent too much time studying others. Doug picked out Prince's athletics, John Lydon's bad posture, and Ozzy Osbourne's flamboyance, just to start. Trevor's flagrant belief in these poses did give the whole act a genuineness, but Doug couldn't help feeling vaguely embarrassed.

"I don't suppose Horror Hospital's destined for great things," he mused aloud. "I don't think there's much chance of that," Frank smiled, as the band, having given the milieu a context, jerked off to the right as though pulled by a hook.

TREVOR BOUGHT THE *Los Angeles Times* at a Quick Shop just up his street. The cashier was used to him, but several customers gawked at his clothes, which were purple today and felt-tipped across the chest with the slogan BEAT UP YOUR CHILD. *He* was a child and the irony there struck two semihip women in Dairy Products.

At home Trevor sat at his parents' dining room table and thumbed through the newspaper. He lit a cigarette as long as his hand. In part four, next to the ad for some movie, a short review was titled "Crash on Course." He skimmed through the usual rave about headliner Darby until he came to a paragraph that read as follows:

Opening the evening was Horror Hospital, a troop of
very young spiky heads who, with a modicum of tech-
nique, treated the usual subjects with typical sneers.
They've got the idea. What they need is maturity and
the finesse that comes with it. For now their sincerity's
almost a reason to sit through them.

Trevor sat back, a little dazed but pleased. He thought
the review had been reasonably worded. His ideas would
be more powerful with age. That made sense. The best
he hoped now was that some intelligence and integrity
showed through. It seemed they did. So the indifference
of people who yawned at his band was okay, then. He
could feel it for what it was.

TREVOR HAD STROLLED by the storefront for years, not
really sure what it was. The windows were painted gray.
So was the rest of its boring facade. There was a red neon
numeral 12 hanging over the door and a condom machine to its right. He doubled back, scrawled the name of
his band on the door with a giant red felt-tip pen.

To 12's immediate left, Rotten Records was having a
sale. Trevor stopped at its show window, eyeing the
Cramps display. Four lifesize cardboard band members
grinned threateningly at the street. Plastic skulls had
been fastened all over their clothes. By the bogus ghouls'
feet lay a fake-looking corpse stuffed with crumpled-up
NME's. Trevor frowned, envious.

Inside he thumbed through the 45's rack, choosing
one single each by Swans, Coil, and Big Black. "Coil!"
squealed the girl at the counter, "Great choice. Hey,
aren't you in . . . what's that band?" "Horror Hospital,"

Trevor chirped. "Yeah, great name," she admitted. "I saw you with Darby at Undo the other night. He's really great, but I thought he was better before he OD'd that last time. Still . . ." She shrugged.

"Look," Trevor said, "what's that place next door?" The girl pretended to gag. "Gay bar. See, listen." She turned down the sound on the store's blaring tape deck. He heard an unmistakable disco beat thump through the wall. "So," she smiled, drowning the thump, "when's, uh, your band coming out with a record?" "Oh, really soon," Trevor lied, "Columbia's *begging* for us."

Leaving the shop, Trevor passed 12 again and continued on. He'd gone two blocks when he figured he might as well scout the place out and turned back. Sometimes his friends and he went to gay bars and let men try to pick them up. The lines gays used were hilarious. He crossed his fingers, walked in. "I'd like a Heineken," he told the bartender.

Luckily 12 had some video games. Unluckily they were Frogger, Ms. Pac Man, and Donkey Kong, the three worst machines on earth. Trevor snarled, put down his beer and his sack of new records, then fished out some change, which included two quarters. He fed them into Frogger and aimed the bright green "toad" across the neon-blue "river."

Boing boing boing. "You like killing those frogs?" asked a voice somewhere near Trevor's shoulder. *Boing boing boing.* "Maybe," he answered. *Boing boing.* "Do you feel like a challenge match?" *Boing boing boing boing.* "Nope." Trevor's quarters ran out. "Piss, shit, fuck, prick."

He seized his beer and leaned back on the Frogger's control panel, fixing his eyes on the emergency exit.

"My name's Tim," said the guy who'd been watching him play, "and you're . . . ?" "Famous," Trevor smirked. He glanced at Tim, who didn't look particularly hip or unhip, smart, dumb, young, old.

"Famous in what way?" Tim asked. Across the room, a balding man about Trevor's dad's age had the pair in his sights. For a laugh Trevor winked in his general direction. The man grinned. "Oh, shit." Trevor clutched Tim's arm. "Uh, I sing in a band and, uh . . . look, pretend I'm your boyfriend, okay? Don't let the old guy get near me. Please? I'll pay you back."

The man positioned himself an inch behind Trevor's back. They could smell how much scotch he'd drunk. He didn't say anything, but Trevor felt the guy's knee between his. Trevor took a step nearer to Tim, who encircled him with his arms. The drunk, seeming to take this display as a signal that Trevor was loose, slipped one hand down the back of his pants.

Trevor spun around. "I'll *totally* kill you!" He punched the man with both fists. While deflecting these blows, the drunk accidentally smacked Trevor's face. Trevor splayed on the Frogger, blood trickling out of his nose. He covered his eyes and tried not to cry. "Asshole!" Tim yelled, shoved the drunk's chest so hard he floored four other men on his way to the wall.

The two stumbled onto the sidewalk, Tim pulling Trevor, who bent forward squeezing his nose to try to stop it from spurting. They ran several blocks before Trevor realized that the best way to cut off the blood was to lie very still somewhere. He yanked his hand out of Tim's and collapsed on his side in a patch of grass.

Tim doubled back. "When the blood stops," he

puffed, kneeling down beside Trevor's head, "we'll go to my place and clean you up. That sound okay?" Passing headlights illuminated Tim's face for a moment. "How old are you?" Trevor asked in a pinched voice. "Eighteen," Tim replied, "and you?" "Eighteen," Trevor said, "why?" Tim shrugged.

TIM SAT AT his folks' kitchen table. From four to six-thirty P.M. it was his desk. His homework was a page of new math and a Spanish I dialogue. The latter textbook was spread to an etching of teenagers smashing piñatas. Tim's eyes were closed. His lips moved. *"Hola, Juan. Hola, Paco. ¡Como estás? Estoy bien, gracias. ¿Y tu? Bien, gracias. ¡Oye, quién es ese chica? Es un amiga mia. ¡Como se llama? Se llama Juanita. . . ."*

He paused, searched his drugged memory for a second. "Oh, fuck this!" Snapping the book shut, he pushed it away.

He ripped a clean page from his notebook and wrote, "Dear Chuck, How are things in Minnesota? Things are fine here. I'm in love with a guy I met. His name is Trevor. I think I've mentioned him. We've been together for over a month now. He's probably bored, since he didn't return my last phone call. But I feel much better than I did a month ago. Other than that I'm getting stoned a lot. . . ."

Tim stopped there, tapping the pen on his cheek. He read the letter back, folded the page into fourths and dropped it into the wastebasket. "Chuck doesn't care," he sighed.

The phone rang. It was Trevor, who wanted to meet and get stoned after Horror Hospital's gig at nine. Tim agreed, hung up, and looked at his watch. Nearly six P.M. He dragged his Spanish book back into range and finished studying just as his mother walked in with the place mats to shoo him away.

After the meal Tim drove downtown to see Trevor's band play at Music Machine, the only half-decent club on the west side. A few kids were standing around the bar. Tim bought a beer, blended in.

Backstage Horror Hospital waited to see if more people would show. At ten-thirty, one and a half hours late, they strolled on. Trevor went to the microphone. "Libation," he said. He closed his eyes for the first several drum beats then yelled what Tim guessed was "My death," and then three other words. Tim couldn't figure them out.

After half an hour of similar songs Trevor announced, "This is the last one. It's called . . ." He looked up at the crowd, which was talking and drinking, oblivious. "Oh, forget it. You don't give a fuck about anything. You're just a bunch of dumb assholes!" He flipped them off. "Show's *over!*" He stormed offstage. The band looked confused for a moment then followed. Three people applauded. Tim loudest.

Tim bought two beers. When he'd paid and was turning to look for a table, Trevor dropped on the stool to his right. "That for me?" He pointed down at the Grolsch. Tim nodded. Trevor drained half the bottle, burped. "We were godlike, I'm sure, but this club attracts assholes, so fuck it."

Trevor looked great in a sweat, Tim thought. So he tested his quietest voice. "Trev?" The boy tilted forward. Tim averted his eyes. "In the mood for some . . . ?" "Sex, huh?" Trevor whispered. He glanced over each of his shoulders then drained the beer. "I feel about sex like I do about lots of things." He smirked at Tim.

Trevor led Tim down a dark hallway whose whole left wall was a mirror. Tim was a few inches taller than Trevor, less pale but more lanky. Trevor glanced at their reflection. He saw Tim was studying them. "You'll get your fill of that"—he jabbed a thumb at his image—"soon."

Tim was tugged through a door marked FOR ARTISTS. Trevor locked it behind them. A toilet dominated the room. No more than three feet from it, a pink sink jutted out of the wall. Tim had to duck, else his head bumped the ceiling. The place smelled of barf.

"Let me undress you," Tim whispered, unzipping Trevor's black jacket, sliding the heavy thing over his hands. He undid his friend's sneakers, unsnapped the jeans, and peeled them with his shorts to his ankles. Trevor stepped out of the wad. His cock was partially hard. His skin was as cold as the sink that he rested against.

Tim wrapped his arms around Trevor. They ogled each other with stupid expressions, like people preparing to kiss. "How far are we going to go with this, Tim?" Trevor asked, peered at Tim's eyes. Tim put his finger-tips to Trevor's cheek like someone checking a bath to see if he could hop in.

A half hour later they sat on the hood of Tim's father's car, sharing a joint while Trevor's band loaded amps and guitars in a van up the block. A few fans stopped by to tell Trevor they liked what they'd seen.

Tim yawned. Trevor patted his friend's head and slid to his feet. They peeked around them, then said their good-byes with a handshake squeezed particularly tight, held unusually long. Tim finished the joint and looked at the stars scattered over the sky. It was pretty up there.

HORROR HOSPITAL GATHERED in Trevor's room. Kim was perched on the edge of the bed. She bunched a throw pillow between her knees and played drums. With her high collar, sans makeup, she looked like a corpse in a coffin. Dull, the jumpy guitarist, fidgeted in one corner. His clothing stank. Bassist Devan, the group's only surfer, did a backstroke across the filthy shag rug. Trevor stepped over him.

He slid a tape into his player, pushed PLAY. For the next several minutes the band listened to its two all-time best numbers, "Tough Luck" and "Libation." "Sounds clean," Dull proclaimed when the tape ended. Kim agreed. Devan held up a fist. "Then you're agreed it's our demo," Trevor said, "and I can send the thing off to Columbia as is?" The others nodded.

"Hey, aren't we supposed to be interviewed by some kind of magazine sometime soon or whatever?" Kim asked. "Yeah, that's right!" Devan yelled, bolting upright. "Have you gotten that thing arranged, Trevor?" Trevor was picking dried mud from the sole of his boot. "Oh, right, I forgot. I'll call them tomorrow." "Bullshit!" Dull hissed.

"If you weren't busy sitting on Tim's face," crowed Devan, "we'd be in the Top Ten by now." "I'm not!" "Sure you are," Devan continued, "you're completely obsessed with sex. You're betraying your own beliefs. You're a hypocrite *and* dumb. Where's the Trevor who wrote, 'Life leaves us frozen in place. / Death is cool and life's a waste'?"

"I still believe that," Trevor protested, crushing a small clod of dried mud between his thumb and forefinger. "Tim's just, like, my personal manager in a way. It's hard to explain. . . . *You* know what it's like, Kim. You were with what's-his-name . . . *Paul* for a year." "Yeah, five years ago, Trevor, when I was a kid. Besides, *you're* a genius and *as* a genius you've got a duty to not waste your talent on *one guy.*"

Trevor shook his head violently. "I—" "When's the last time you wrote a song?" Dull interrupted. "Yesterday." "Sure, let's hear it!" Trevor whipped something out of his pants pocket. "Okay, imagine this," he said quickly, "you guys are making some horrible feedback and stuff. I'm lit from below. You play awhile, then I start to chant. . . ."

The members leaned forward. Trevor closed his eyes and pinched the bridge of his nose, getting into Machine mood. Once he reopened them they wore a coldly determined expression, not self-involved or unfriendly exactly, but spooky to people who knew him nonetheless. "I think it's possible," he read, "to die/without dying exactly. It's shit here/I know, but it's worse there, wherever . . ."

Devan cocked his head. Dull squinted. Kim stared vacuously at a wall. When their leader finished reciting the lyric, they praised it and tried to describe the feedback they'd formulate underneath. Trevor got Cokes from the fridge and they listened to three Butthole Surfers LP's in a row. Then they made an appointment to practice before their next gig.

At the end of the driveway Dull, Devan, and Kim formed a huddle. "What did you honestly think of the words?" Dull asked. "I don't know," Devan said, "they're so . . ." "Esoteric," Kim snapped, "too stylized, too Doors, not real, not us." "God, I hope he pops out of this," Dull muttered. "Look, for the next gig at least," Kim suggested, "let's drown Trevor out on the new song, okay?" The others nodded.

Just then Tim drove up, parked, walked down the driveway, waved to the band, and rang the doorbell. Trevor practically squealed with delight when he opened the door. Tim went inside. "I wonder what it would be like," Dull mused, "to sleep with Trevor." "I can tell you that," Devan yawned. Kim and Dull: "*What?!*" "Yeah, back when Trevor and I were in junior high he stayed at my place one night.

"It's bizarre," he went on, "because Trevor's a genius and all, but the sex was a bore. You'd think it would be a spiritual experience, I know. He just sort of lay there. Besides, his body's built kind of weird and his penis is too long and veiny. . . ." "Stop!" Dull yelled. He covered his ears with his hands.

"MISS CLARK," ANNOUNCED Jerry Sands, A&R man for Columbia Records, "please bring in today's batch of demos. Thanks." He put down the phone, swiveled around in his chair. His eyes strayed to the opposite wall with its dozen framed platinum records. Midday light through a window behind him made them appear three-dimensional like giant, piss-flavored Life Savers. "Ugh." He did a hit of coke. Sniff, sniff.

Miss Clark dropped a half-dozen large, bulky envelopes onto his desk. Jerry waved her away. As she strode off he eyed her ass and made a mental note: "Ask her out next chance." He automatically reached in a drawer for his vial of coke, but, unscrewing the cap for the nth time that day, he asked himself if he wasn't already too high. "Oh, half a hit," he thought. Sniff.

He tore open the envelopes one by one. Each contained a glossy photo, a cassette tape, and a few pages stapled together. To save time he'd taught himself how to recognize talented bands or performers from how they'd posed. For example, the first packet came from a woman whose facial expression spoke volumes. "Yuppie, soft soul, CD audience. The market's flooded." She hit the trash.

Next was a country-rock outfit ("*Jee*-zus!") then a couple of hip-hop groups ("That's over."). The final photograph caught Jerry's eye for two reasons. First, the band looked ridiculous. Secondly, he thought the boy on the left was a beautiful girl at first. "Horror Hospital?!" Turned out the girl on the right was a boy and the boy to his left a girl. "Huh?" Jerry tried the accompanying letter.

It was full of inept, contrived rage and self-important pronouncements, most of which held an unintentional charm, at least to someone on coke. "Maybe," Jerry decided, "they're some kind of speed-metal offshoot. That sells. Could these kids be the Wham of hard rock? I should check them out, take Miss Clark . . . hmm . . ." He did two more spoonfuls of coke.

Crossing the room, he fixed his haircut and tie before the platinum disk that he used as a mirror. By sheer coincidence it was Bad Company's *Greatest Hits*. He knew he looked sort of clichéd. Still, he realized that if he thought anymore about what he was doing, it would mean going back into therapy. "Don't think, behave," he said, forcing a sarcastic smile to his sweaty face. "Yeah, *that's* Jerry Sands."

* * *

BACKSTAGE AT OLIO, Trevor sat on a folding chair getting into Machine mood. The other band members roamed through the tiny club looking for dealers or friends. Brainless Wonder, a syntho-gloom duo scheduled to headline the show, were in the dressing room's toilet stall shooting up. One of them had just wrecked Trevor's concentration by nodding out or OD'ing or something equally old school.

Suddenly Dull rushed in, grabbed and shook Trevor's shoulders. "You won't believe this!" Trevor reluctantly opened his eyes. "Believe what?" "An A&R man from Columbia Records is out there to see us play!" Trevor blinked. Brainless Wonder came staggering out of the toilet stall. "Columbia Records," one slurred, "where?" "To see *us!*" Dull shouted. Trevor clutched his guitarist's arm. "Get the group back here quick!"

While Dull corralled the band, Trevor attempted to grin all the happiness out of his system. If he went onstage in this state of mind, he'd definitely seem pseudo-dark. "Disaster." He jumped to his feet and started bouncing around like a boxer. That tired him out a bit. Then he took a long look at Brainless Wonder spasming on the floor. "Think pathetic," he urged himself.

Horror Hospital clustered around their lead singer. He advised them to try even harder than usual to stay in tune and keep the chords to the different songs straight. "Just look pissed and concentrate on our future, okay?" Dull bit his cuticles. Devan farted. Trevor hugged Kim, who had always been his favorite drummer, for luck.

"Trevor Jones? There's a call for you." A club employee had entered the room. He stood waiting to lead whoever answered away. "It must be my mom," Trevor groaned. He pried himself off of Kim. "I'll be right back. Psych yourselves up . . . I mean *down*, guys." He followed the gofer, whose ass looked exactly like Tim's, up a steep flight of stairs. "You can talk in that office there."

Trevor picked up the phone. "God speaking," he joked. "Trevor Jones?" asked a female voice he didn't recognize. "Sure." "I'm the mother of Tim Wilson," she said. "Oh, hi," Trevor giggled, "he hasn't shown up here yet. Want me to have him call?" "No," said the woman, "Tim was killed in a traffic accident this afternoon. We thought you should know." Trevor put down the phone. A moment later Dull banged on the door and yelled, "We're on!"

JERRY STUDIED THE crowd from a small, ringside table. "These kids can't afford to buy records," he muttered. Miss Clark looked amazingly chic if out of place in her beige Kawakubo "dress." She flinched every time a "young witch," as she'd termed the punk women, came within two or three feet. "Think of them as our shadows," he cooed, "flickering in candlelight, dancing on bedroom walls. . . ." She nodded, grimaced.

"One-two-three, one-two-three." A balding teenaged boy had commandeered the stage. Jerry squeezed Miss Clark's hand, then inhaled a quick spoonful of coke. Sniff. "Hi, I'm the brilliant entrepreneur who runs Olio," said the announcer, "and here's a band whom I like fairly well. Horror Hospital." There was some cursory applause, then the kids Jerry knew from the photo trooped out.

One of them tore the microphone right off its stand. His eyes were puffy and wet. "I just heard some bad news and I hate all you fucking shits! You're just fucking *nothing!* I just . . ." The band began their first number. The flustered singer dropped to his knees and threw the microphone across the stage. His body trembled and swayed out of time with the music.

Jerry nuzzled Miss Clark. "Well," he yelled in her ear, "this is rather amusing. I think he's doing a punk James Brown revue type of thing. It's a new one on me. There's a freshness, for sure. But how to get it on vinyl? See, that's the question. You'd lose all their humor, I think. And unfortunately the music's bullshit."

The song fell apart. The singer crawled to his microphone, held it up, and blubbered, "I'm the one who should die. All you fucking assholes know it. I want to *die* . . ." His words deteriorated in sobs. The other band members glanced at one another. One started to play and the others joined in. It could have been a new song or the first one again.

"It's too Johnny-one-note," Jerry yelled. "For a concept like this to work you've got to pace it like clockwork. Remember the Tubes? They were an excellent band. But their records sold shit. Couldn't capture their comic genius on vinyl. No, the 'horror' is wearing off. I'll give them two minutes flat to change my mind, or . . ." He glued his mouth to Miss Clark's.

Their tongues sloshed together for several minutes. "Let's . . . go . . . home," he wheezed. She fanned herself with the ashtray. He did a smidgen more coke, then helped his date up from her chair. As they stood, his eyes strayed to the band. "I want to d-i-e!" the boy singer screeched. Jerry raised one arm, made a pistol-shaped fist, and aimed it generally at Trevor. "Bang."

(1984)

HE CRIED

IT'S A GREAT day, but Craig's indoors clipping out part of the newspaper. Cops have found some more nude mutilated boys. Four death masks frame a short article. They are the seventh, eighth, ninth, and tenth victims of an unusually savage serial murderer. They were thirteen, fourteen, eighteen, and twenty-two. Their completely expressionless faces amaze Craig and give him chills he can't account for. He knows it's a dumb rationale to say his interest in them is aesthetic, though he once claimed as his favorite work of art "a lukewarm corpse after rigor mortis has passed, before the stench inherent in such a romantic notion sets in." It just popped out.

He drives into Riverside and drops the clipping at Photo Impact. He has coffee just down the street, then picks up his 3 × 5 enlargement. He tacks it next to the others across his bedroom wall. Ten corpses stare through the grain like hallucinations he used to worry he'd never come down from. They're nothing new. Since childhood he has been blowing up pictures of people in order to scrutinize them, not for suspiciously misshapen wounds like cops would, but more in the way he used to peer at the river near his parents' mansion, sure it held passages to wilder places. Not that he's found anything police could use during an investigation. Not that he's found much at all, but he's drawn to them.

Take John Doe #4, discovered facedown in a stream, naked except for a red bandanna. On shore, his bright blue pup tent and cooking gear were as curtly arranged as an advertisement, and under a nearby tree, officers found a Styx T-shirt drenched with blood. It was peeking through some tall grass. John had long blond hair, was in his early teens, had pale blue eyes, was five feet nine inches tall, weighed 120 pounds. He had been sodomized, beaten, and killed by a number of stabs in the back. In Craig's enlargement, he looks like a kid who, interrupted mid-masturbation by knocks at his bedroom door, shuts his eyes, hoping to appear to be sleeping when Dad peers in. But his face looks too intent on sleep, and any dad would get wind of the truth and simply tiptoe away. Craig doesn't get wind of very much in John's features. He just feels in awe of how shallow and edgy John's death seems.

He remembers a dream he had where the dumb-looking John Doe #6 crouched on a skateboard rattling down a steep street in his old neighborhood. Doe never reached bottom. Somebody drove up alongside and offered a ride that the boy agreed to with such bored stoicism he could have passed for a midget at that moment, except he was physically splendid and his stern Mexican face was unlined by pain. Craig was catching some rays in his front yard when he noticed Doe strolling back up the hill, skateboard under one arm. The kid was no more pale, sunken, or reserved than before, but Craig just knew he'd been raped and murdered by the shadowy driver.

Craig yelled, "Hey, *you*," and Doe changed direction, heading for him. They ended up face to face by the river. Craig had to make elaborate signs with his hands to communicate with the kid, and Doe barely nodded yes or no in return, never shifting his yellowy, seemingly hypnotized eyes. Guessing Doe was in his total power, and knowing the kid had been sodomized anyway, Craig was about to suggest a quick round of strip poker when his companion made a strange noise and fell backward, *really* dead. Craig was rolling Doe into the river and giving frantic looks over his shoulder, sure cops were going to arrest him, when he sat straight up in bed.

(1983)

WRONG

WHEN MIKE SAW a pretty face, he liked to mess it up, or give it drugs until it wore out by itself. Take Keith, who used to play pool at the Ninth Circle. His crooked smile really lights up the place. That's what Mike heard, but it bored him. "Too obvious."

Keith was a kiss-up. Mike fucked him hard, then they snorted some dope. Keith was face first in the toilet bowl when Mike walked in. Keith had said, "Knock me around." But first Mike wanted him "dead." Not in the classic sense. "Passed out."

Mike dragged Keith down the hall by his hair. He shit in Keith's mouth. He laid a whip on Keith's ass. It was a grass skirt once Mike dropped the belt. Mike kicked Keith's skull in before he came to. Brains or whatever it was gushed out. "That's that."

José was Keith's friend. Now that Keith wasn't around he moved in. Mike said okay *if* they'd fist fuck. José's requirement was drugs: speed, coke, pot, the occasional

63

six-pack. "Oh, and respect, of course."

"Great stuff," José whispered. Mike shrugged. "Too fem," he thought, putting a match to José's pipe. José had hitchhiked from Dallas. He had a high-pitched voice, wore a gold crucifix on a chain. "Typical Mexican shit."

José slipped on a dress. Pink satin, ankle length, blue sash. He put on makeup. *"Mamacita!"* Mike fisted "her" on the window ledge. "She" dangled over the edge. Mike shook "her" off his wrist. "She" fell four stories, broke "her" neck.

Steve had blond hair, gloomy eyes, and chapped lips. "He should be dead," Mike thought. He liked the kid's skin, especially on his ass. Sick white crisscrossed with gray stretch marks. Mike liked how lost it became in pants, like the bones in an old lady's face.

Mike knocked a few of Steve's teeth out. He'd called Mike "a dumb fuck." That night Mike kicked in Steve's ribs and tied him up for the night. They fell asleep around four. By morning Steve was cold, eyes open, blue face. Mike dressed and took off.

He walked home. He thought of offing himself. "After death, what's left?" he mumbled. He meant "to do." Once you've killed someone, life's shit. It's a few rules and you've already broken the best. He had a beer at the Ninth Circle.

He picked up Will on the street. "Snort this." Mike tore Will's shorts off and slapped his ass. "Shit in my mouth," Mike said. Will did. It changed the way Mike perceived him. Will was a real person, not just a fuck. Mike let him hang out.

Will's body came into focus. It wasn't bad: underweight, blue eyes, a five o'clock shadow. Beauty had nothing to do with it. Mike could see what he was look-

ing at. But he got used to the sight. One night he strangled Will to be safe.

The night was rough: wind, rain, chill. Mike walked
from Will's place on West Tenth to Battery Park, chains
clinking each step. He stared out at the Hudson. He put
a handgun to his head. "Fuck this shit." His body
splashed in the river, drifted off.

Morning came. Cops kicked Will's door in, found his
corpse. Will's friends got wind of it, phoned one another
up. Down river tourists were standing around on a dock
looking bored. One girl pulled down on her mom's skirt
and pointed out. "What's that?"

GEORGE LOOKED OUT at the Hudson. He saw a dead body.
He shot the rest of his roll of film, then milled around
with the other tourists. Guides led them back to the bus.
It was abuzz with the idea of death, in grim or joking
tones. George listened, his feelings somewhere between
the two.

The World Trade Center was not what he'd hoped. It
wasn't like he could fall off. Big slabs of glass between
him and his death. No matter where he turned his
thoughts were obvious. The city looked like a toy, a
space-age forest, a silvery tray full of hypodermics. He
wanted one fresh perception, but . . .

Wall Street was packed with gray business suits. Seeing the trading floor, he thought first of a beehive, then
of the heart attacks those guys would get. It was like
watching a film about some other time and place, very
far back and relegated to books.

George took off his clothes. He lay on the bed. "Where
you from?" It was his roommate, a Southerner, judging

by the accent. "West." "Of what?" the man asked.
"This," and George turned his back. The Southerner
shook his head. "Not worth it," he thought.

That night George walked through the West Village.
"I'm tired of sleeping with *that*," a man sneered as they
crossed paths. The guy was chatting to some friend of
his, but he eyed George's ass. Hearing this, George felt
as cold as the statue he'd touched at the Met last night.
A boy was playing the lute when art froze him stiff.

The Ninth Circle was packed. Hustlers in blue jean
vests, businessmen in all the usual suits. George leaned
against the bar lighting a cigarette. "What's up pal?" It
was his roommate's voice. "Not much," George
thought, but they talked.

Lights out. Dan's cock was minuscule, so George
agreed to be fucked. Dan spread the asscheeks and
sniffed. George did his best to relax. He thought of ovens
with roasts cooking in them. He knew his ass smelled
more rancid than them, but maybe that was the point.

George thought of home. It was a white stucco, one
story. His room was paneled in oak. He never aired it
out. It reeked of BO, smoke, and unlaundered sheets.
The smell was clinically bad, but he loved the idea that
he'd had such an impact on something outside himself.

George didn't want to be held while he slept. He never
got enough rest as it was. No lover could comprehend
that. To them a hug was an integral act. George felt
pinned down by one, too pressed to squeeze back.
"Don't." Dan sighed and moved off.

George dreamed in bursts. Little picturesque plots.
Casts of peripherals refocused, brought to the fore in a
world he'd backed into unknowingly. He saw himself
floating dead in the Hudson; Dan held a knife to his

throat in an alley; the room caught fire and he went up in smoke.

Dan thought of love as defined by books, cobwebbed and hidden from view by the past. Too bad a love like that didn't actually exist. In the twentieth century one had to fake it. He put his cheek on the boy's ass and seemed to sleep. He couldn't tell if he was or not. Then he did.

GEORGE SAT ON a park bench feeding some birds what was left of his sandwich. He drew a handful of postcards from one jacket pocket. They were all cityscapes, what friends and folks would expect. Bums limped by begging for change. Their clothes were falling off. George turned his palms up. "Die," he said under his breath.

"Dear Philippe, New York makes sense. I fit right in. I'm sitting under a bunch of trees. They'd be great if bums weren't dying all over the place. Everything you said was right. I'm going back to the hotel now to take a nap. Anyway, George."

"Dear Dad, The trip's going great. We're in New York for the weekend, then up to Boston, then the ride back to L.A. The man I'm sharing a room with reminds me of you. He's nice, from the South. Don't touch a thing in my room. I'll be home in two weeks. Love, George."

"Dear Sally, I thought about you today as I walked forty blocks to a pretty park. My legs are used to it. They sell marijuana in stores here. I bought a bag for ten bucks. I'm smoking it as I write. Out of room. Be seeing you in awhile. Love, George."

"Dear Santa Claus, For Christmas I want a penthouse in New York, one in L.A., and one someplace in Europe.

I've been a good boy, plus . . ." George ripped the card in half. "Duh," he said, giggling at himself.

"Dear Dennis, I think I miss you most of all. What's-her-name said that to Ray Bolger, right? Yesterday I saw the top of what's on this card. Today I'm off on my own. Tonight I'll hit the bars. Hope you're great. See you, George."

George headed toward the hotel. His calves ached. Times Square was spooky; too many junkies out, pissed eyes way back in their heads. The hotel lobby felt homey. Dan was out. George kicked his shoes off, snoozed a bit.

The Ninth Circle was packed. George downed three beers in no time. One man was cute, but his haircut resembled a toupee. Another stood in an overhead light, too sure of its effect. His expression was "perfect." Between them George would have chosen the latter, depending on who else showed up.

Fred's loft was spacious, underfurnished. Track lighting bleached out its lesser points. George got the grand tour. "This is the bed, of course. This is a painting by Lichtenstein. Amusing, yes? And these are the torture devices I mentioned." George saw a long table lined with spiked dildos, all lengths of whips, three branding irons, sundry shit.

To George it looked like a game. Whether it wound up that way or not was beside the point. Handcuffs clicked shut in the small of his back. Electrical tape sealed his lips. Black leather shorts made him feel sort of animal-esque.

George fantasized that his father was hugging him. He didn't know why. It had something to do with a gesture that couldn't be downgraded or reinterpreted, made into some half-assed joke. Someone who made him feel this all important must be intrigued at least.

It started out with a spanking. Slaps to the face, which George wasn't so wild about. His asshole swallowed in something's enormity simply enough. More slaps. Fred's breaths grew worse, a kind of storm knocking down every civilized word in its path.

George was hit on the head. "Shit!" Again. This time he felt his nose skid across one cheek. His forehead caved in. One eye went black. Teeth sputtered out of his mouth and rained down on his chest. He died at some point in that.

GEORGE WAS ACROSS the loft watching himself kick. The sight was slightly blurred like the particulars in a dream sequence. He saw a club strike his face. It was unrecognizable. His arms and legs slammed the tabletop like giant crudely made gavels.

George had a lump in his throat. He wondered why, if he was still alive, he should feel shit for that too-garish wreck of himself. "But that's the beauty of dead kids," he thought. "Everything they ever did seems incredibly moving in retrospect."

He watched until his old body was such a loss that each indignity was simply more of the same. So he looked down at his current form. He was a hologram, more or less. "Too much!" he thought. He tried to walk. It was a snap, like bounding over the moon.

So this was death. "Hey, not bad," he thought. He inhaled slowly and slid without incident through the steel door. Descending the stairs was exactly like falling down them, liberated and discombobulating, a drug hallucination without the teeth grinding.

He walked west, sometimes right down the middle of streets, cars plowing through him. He strolled through shoppers, amused by the idea that he was just part of the air to them, at best a breeze they'd write off to earth's natural forces.

Seeing a husband and wife, the male of which he'd have been quite attracted to during his life, he followed them up a rickety staircase, through their front door. Jeff, as the wife called him, hit the head. George watched him shit, loved the dumb look on his face, but was driven back into the street by the subsequent stench.

Now what? He took a leisurely stroll to the river, down Christopher Street. The piers were decrepit. One was completely decapitated. A few rotten pylons stuck out of the water. George felt an odd emotional attachment to them.

He sat on a bench. The dawn felt terrific. He warmed slightly like fog just before it burned off. He thought of movies he'd loved where the ghosts of dead men were big jokes, mere plot twists, a sort of stab in the dark.

Who would have thought it was true? All those old ladies in New England mansions were far more sane than their distended eyes would have had one believe. "One," he muttered. He'd always hated when people used "one" in conversation. But it was the right term for him now.

He stared out at the brownish river. It was the first time he'd thought about water's solidity. If he were to hurl himself in, would he break into millions of molecules? Or would he, like Jesus Christ, land on his feet? "Interesting prospect," he thought, but he couldn't chance it.

He walked slowly up West Street past several leather
bars he would have liked to check into, but he was tired.
Sure, he could crash out wherever he liked, see which-
ever cute rock star nude, fly to London for nothing. But
he'd get bored of the voyeur bit before he knew it. Then
what?

George thought of things that had haunted him during
his life: A staircase that, after turning a corner, led to a
brick wall. B&W photos of great buildings destined to be
dusty heaps. A human face that had turned into just one
more mudslide from heaven.

The hotel loomed in the distance. Its neon sign
blinked out VACANCY. "An appropriate place for myself
or what's left of me," George thought. He headed for its
rococo, checking the faces of hapless pedestrians for his
reflection. But they stared straight ahead, not realizing.

GEORGE PASSED THROUGH the door of room 531. Dan lay
on the single bed nearest the window, writing a postcard,
probably to the wife he'd been complaining about on the
previous night. His face seemed peaceful, but maybe it
was the light: low, grayish.

George liked Dan, though "liked" was too clear a
word. "Something" had drawn George to him. It had to
do with Dan's fatherliness, George thought. That was a
much bigger turn-on than tight jeans on tanned, overex-
ercised guys. His ideal man was a little bushed around
the eyes.

George hadn't spoken all day. He felt a tightness inside his throat. "Dan?" he croaked, "I know you don't
hear me, but if you can sense me in any way tug on your
left ear." George waited. Dan continued to scratch out

what George had no doubt were inanities.

"Okay, I feel a little like somebody telling some guy in a coma I still care, but here goes. I don't really know you, but I feel attached to you, even though you're not exactly an individual. You're more a type, which makes me some kind of aesthete, I guess, and you the real work of art, not that I buy all your bullshit.

"We had sex. I let you fuck me. That was the hot part, but though it's hard to admit, all the hugging and shit is what I really liked. To be held tight by a person who's had me . . . well it's one thing to shake hands and chat awkwardly about art, and something else to be fucked then respected.

"I used to think that if lovers got wind of my shit I'd be 'too realistic,' in their words. I kept rolling onto my back, clenching my ass when sucked off so the stink couldn't get out. I had this weird idea that there was something wrong under my looks, not just gory stuff.

"Then some guy ate out my ass and asked for a second date. Since that night I've tried to shrug off each fear in turn. Now I'm dead. It figures no one's around to appreciate or make bad jokes about my 'passing on,' as you'd probably call it.

"I wanted love. Sure, I was attracted to sex-crazed types, their faces so overcome by the need for me it was as though leers were sculpted right into their skulls and their skin was just draped over bone like a piece of cloth. But I was a stupid jerk.

"This part is meant for my father's ears. I've felt more than you thought or I'm able to spit out. My moods were really mysterious, even to me, which makes them not worth the time to you, no matter how long you stared in my 'great eyes' last night."

George felt faint and teetered slightly. He wished he had a banana, something with sugar to pep him up, but he imagined he couldn't eat, that food would perch in his waist like a caged canary, or drop with a thump to the carpet.

Dan filled the postcard and lay back. George could just make it out. "Dear Fran," it began. He didn't notice his name in the scribbles. It was a simple tale: Empire State Building, good view, dinner at Lüchow's, Love, Dan. P.S. I wish (unintelligible) tonight.

Was George beginning to fade away? He wasn't sure. So much depended on the right light. "Umm, this may be it," he mumbled. He hadn't meant to lower his voice. "Shit," and he started to tremble. "I like you. What can I say? Or not you, but you're all I have.

"I blew it." He blended into the afternoon. Outside the window a car honked. Inside the room a man's watch ticked. Dan stood and scratched his ass. He put the card in his shirt pocket. He had a faraway look in his eyes as he lit his cigarette.

(1986)

DINNER

"WHAT A BEAUTIFUL ass," said the man with the brown mustache to the man with the blond one. ". . . like the Blarney Stone or a chunk of the Wailing Wall. I'd like to fall there and . . ." What he meant to say: Here was an ass he'd love to find in his bed, lift up the sheet like a tent flap on heaven, and feel it there, peaceful and warm.

Tom had driven by Paul's Bar for years. Recently he'd heard via gossip at college that it had a gay clientele. Tonight he'd been in the dorm room, trying to forget a blond hunk in his geography class. He'd grown pissed at himself for just sitting there jerking off and, in that anger's slight bravery, drove here.

The bar was crowded, but, scanning its realm, Tom couldn't see anyone his age. He'd hoped he would see someone from college, a guy he had wondered about. Not even male cheerleaders were here, though a handful of guys on the small, strobing dance floor had their backs to him and might wind up familiar when they whirled around.

"I want him," stated the brown mustache to the blond one, after panning their quarters once more to make sure there was no competition. His eyes lounged on Tom.

"Yeah," the blond smirked, "you and the legions." He pointed there, there, and there at men ogling.

"I have my powers," smiled the brunet, and he sauntered in Tom's direction.

A few dances later, Tom followed his partner into the parking lot, toward a white Cadillac off by itself at the back of the building, near its trash bins. He couldn't tell for sure in the dark, but the car's windows looked tinted.

The man unlocked the door, opened it, gestured inside. Tom stepped past the polite, chauffeurlike posture, the extended arm, the pointing hand, and slid across the velour backseat to the opposite side. His foot hit a bottle of something down on the floor. The man climbed in after, reached over to make sure the locks were secure on both doors. Then he fumbled down by the young man's feet and came up with the bottle.

"Some vodka?" He tipped it at Tom.

They traded it back and forth while the man scrutinized, and Tom tried to look casual. When the bottle was empty, there was nothing between them.

The man tongued Tom's ear. "Let's get your pants off," he whispered.

Tom lifted his hips. The man pulled the jeans down. He ripped off the tennies, then Tom reached down, peeled his own socks.

He felt the man's mouth on his cock, which was still only semierect. "This should get it hard for sure," he thought. But the man did everything this side of biting it off and it still drooped away.

The man relaxed a few seconds, kissing the softening

penis, absentmindedly rubbing Tom's legs. He wondered whether to try and give the boy pleasure in some other way, or just go ahead with his game plan. The kid was an angel. He had long, hairy legs and was practically porcelain everywhere else. The body was trim and, glancing up at Tom's eyes, which were looking somewhere else, thinking impenetrable things, he confirmed how pretty the face was.

"Okay. Why don't you get on your hands and knees, facing your window. Do you know the position I mean?"

Feeling calm now, Tom pulled off his shirt. "Sure." He shifted until he felt comfortable, pressed one hand flat to the seat pad below and one to the side of the car. "Like this?"

He felt the man's hands on the soles of his feet, working their way up his calves, thighs, crack, combing those fields for his soft spot. His forehead rested against the window. Looking outside, he saw a man walk alone to a car and unlock its door. The small inner lights made it seem warmly intricate there, like a carnival seen from a distance. The stranger folded away inside it. He and it darkened. The car glided away.

Tom stared at the trash cans. A Kellogg's Corn Flakes box had fallen out. He gazed at the untended back of the building as carefully as he imagined anyone ever had, aside from its architect.

The man ran his hands up the boy's legs. The handsome young face was away, and the man had only this form to admire, with his impression of the boy's looks, their possible expression, to give the torso importance enough to do what he wanted. The ass was impeccable. The man would kiss here without having to worry about its opinion. Nothing would watch him or pull back or twitch beyond recognition. The boy was as distant from these moves as God from His priests down on earth.

Tom stared at but didn't see the armrest. He flipped the ashtray lid open and shut unthinkingly. He'd come around. This felt sexy. He looked back over his shoulder. At the end of his back, the man's haughty veneer had become ugly and hyperactive. The eyes bugged. Everything on his face sloped, like the sides of a volcano, out to the mouth. It reminded Tom of the face of a desperate swimmer he'd once felt clawing by in the ocean, flailing up toward fresh air.

He turned to the window again. His cock was hard and one of his hands pumped it harder. He could imagine the blond in his class was behind him, doing this with eyes as fierce and tongue as sharp as a lion's.

The smoky glass was a voluptuous white with Tom's breath. He licked it away, kept tonguing the glass, the upholstery, bit the armrest so hard that stuffing showed in his teethmarks.

The man was up on his knees now, slapping Tom's ass as if it were OD'ing, fucking it with three greasy fingers, twisting the balls like the rotary on a toy airplane. Both the men's breaths blew in ever-altering rhythms, manned by the shapes of words that, because of the distance between them, neither could quite comprehend.

Tom's head bumped the window over and over. He was dreaming of two or three guys back there on his ass, all of them crazy for him, having been lowered to that. He pushed his tongue out as far as it reached, licked all around his big lips.

The boy's ass was as red as a stoplight. The man wanted farther inside. He unfolded a palm from his cock, fished the popper out of his shirt pocket, reached under Tom's nose and cracked it.

"Sniff hard."

The boy did, until his upper legs tensed, which showed it had worked. Now the man churned three fingers deeper into the well-stretched-out hole, withdrew them a little, and pushed four back in. He squeezed the thumb up. Then he dialed and dialed until his hand was enclosed. The anus handcuffed his wrist. The boy was breathing so deeply the man thought that he might be dangerous or in danger.

Suddenly, Tom shot off on his fingers. His body shuddered. His head clunked forward against the glass.

Now the man worked his own cock, concentrating his thoughts on the fact that his hand was inside of a beautiful body. Immediately he came on the seat. Then he screwed his hand out. His breathing slowed to its usual tempo. He looked at what he had done.

"Sit up, okay?" he asked.

Tom obeyed.

The man eyed the boy's face impassively, as he might a Miss California contestant. He felt like he'd just held it under some water until it confessed what he'd needed. What beauty it held was deeper set than its bones now, plowed under all the man's knowledge.

Tom reached for his clothes and started untangling, wiping his hands with the wad of them, swabbing his neck.

The man gripped Tom's shoulder, said, "Put on your things and take off. I'm going for a walk." Then he opened the door and was gone, in a roll of the evening's air that covered Tom's body with goose bumps, until the door slammed.

(1980)

SQUARE ONE

In a recent issue of *Art News*, painter David Salle is quoted as saying most artists he knows are obsessed with pornography. Certainly Salle's early canvases, with their cartoonish spread-beaver shots, reflect this interest, as do crucial works by his immediate contemporaries: Fischl's nudes traipsing down neo-beaches, Rothenberg's icons with hard-ons, Clemente's slithering, farting self-portraits, for instance. Concurrently, the sharpest new writers tend to appropriate either the language or sheen of pornography: Acker in general, Gluck's stories and novels, ditto Killian, (Boyd) McDonald's "found" *Straight to Hell* chronicles. . . . In fact, significant artists in just about every form seem familiar with porn. Foreman, Cronenberg, Lynch, Finley, etc. Their plays, films, performances formulate an aesthetic side to the erotic but remain works of art, loyal to headstrong principles.

Pornography, on the other hand, can be pure documentation and art simultaneously. Take its basic structure—

81

the introduction of characters, interaction, seduction, nudity, sexual encounter, climax, separation. In larger doses this format's so boring that voyeurs must learn to perceive it cleverly. So, slight discrepancies in lighting, say, or oblivious camera angles, bad overdubbing, the shadows of crew and director—all are paramount. Collectively they imbue what seems simplistic with extra-added dimension. Serious students of porn apply the same rigorous mind-set to their favorite medium as conventional aesthetes apply to an exhibition of paintings, enjoying the pleasures of flesh as the latter do the properties of paint, judging and contextualizing a movie's ulterior components according to similarly deduced rules of thumb.

Just as contemporary art eschews the traditional notion of subject, relying instead on a display of purely aesthetic components, pornography's not about what it appears to observe—sex. Porn's simply intimate with human beings, its components, though not necessarily the stars of the movie one's watching. They're just the wardrobes sex happens to wear on particular outings. And, like clothes worn by fashion models, they may be the highlight in each frame of film, but they're hardly porn's real subject. That subject is lust—theirs, their director's, their viewers'. Without it, porn films would be as sterile as fashion layouts, its actors mere mannequins, signifiers, and not a liberating army inspired by porn's lack of rules.

Choosing a star suitable to his tastes, a soon-to-be-liberated man enters a porn theater, sits down, watches the star be explored and exploited by co-stars. He pictures himself in one or more of these go-betweens' places. He calls up memories of his own measly sex life to create tastes, smells, textures for the star's body. While the go-betweens suck, rim, and fuck (or are sucked, rimmed, and fucked by) the star, this viewer's mind drifts down the trail blazed for him. An audience made up of men like me has surrendered its collective will to a filmmaker's. Like a cheap spaceship prop in an old sci-fi flick, a grungy theater scattered with hopeful upturned faces seems to speed toward its destination— giant bodies composed of light.

My particular destination is a young man with short brown hair named Jeff Hunter, star of a half-dozen videos and films (*Pacific Coast Highway, Kept After School, The Come On,* etc.). His physical makeup fits my master plan for the "ideal sex partner," a guy I've refined from my fifteen or more years of fucking and fantasizing. His personality's vaguely discernible—lazy, good-humored, passive, self-absorbed. Jeff exists to have sex, in particular suck cock, rim, get rimmed, get fucked. He appeared on the earth in his late teens and disappeared late in his twenties. The peak of his life occurs midway through *Kept After School.* He's standing spread-legged in a classroom set. One man eats out his ass, another sucks his cock, a third licks his balls, a fourth french-kisses him. Never again will his face be as gripped by what's deep in his body but slipping from his possession.

I've focused on Jeff, but what I'm thinking about is how he must have felt having sex in such a transparent context. I'm an aesthete looking closely at a metaphorical window as though it were actually open. I use it to spy on a scene that exists for my benefit yet over which I have zero control. I've half resigned myself to simply scratching its surface. I concede that my separation from it is an intricate part of its magic. Its magic is an abstraction a cute guy like Jeff can stand around naked in, feeling more important than he could realistically be, despite the number of men paid or paying to see him, no matter how hard an artwork has tried to edit him down to perfection, nor how great a hand he may have in its highness.

WHEN I THINK of Jeff Hunter, I see him eighteen years old, the year we "met." I picked him out of the cast of *Pacific Coast Highway*. A muscular man fucked his brains out, then drove away in a van. Jeff hung around in the foggy light awhile, thinking back, jerking off. Loner type. He made that work for a few years, quit porn, wrinkled up, OD'd, tested positive for AIDS . . . who knows? I'm catching up with what I missed, the occasional loop. Last week I bought a porn magazine, brought it home, jerked off three nights in a row before I realized it was Jeff being fist-fucked on page seventeen. He'd been folded into a grotesque shape by three older men. I could see about a third of his vaguely Germanic face. His nose seemed newly broken. His eyes looked like the bottoms of old coffee cups. There was a definite smudge over whatever lust was still smoldering out back.

   It's not Jeff who moves me, like I said. He's the part I can relate to. It's as though some concept way over my head has taken human form so we can communicate, like aliens did in B films that I realized were shit back when I was probably too young to judge. It's as if Jeff is moaning, "This is as much as you'll grasp," and not, "Fuck me," continuously. He's a warped person, but I keep sneaking back into the rickety storefronts where his films are booked. I try to read something into what little

I manage to glimpse by the light of the hard-on I hold out. "Why's he so hot?" I write down in my notebook, then, later, "Resemblance." That means George M., long-lost friend, and Jeff look-alike. He was sixteen. I was eighteen, tops. I supplied drugs. He took his clothes off, lay back on my bed, and smiled into my camera lens. Click.

George was the most focused part of what I'd fashioned into a sex life in '71. It was he I imagined my cock entering each night, not just his flimsy ass, though that's the first thing I opened when I got the chance. The smooth, shiny pages of magazines seem to encompass the world when you're young or have given up looking for someone to fuck for the night. I shut my eyes. His used to shimmer, no matter how glazed they got. I had no idea how small a part of his life they were letting me in on. I couldn't do anything for him, it turned out. Keep telling yourself that. I flipped the page. Jeff came in some clone's mouth. George quit school, took off. I've lost track of what I felt.

Sometimes pornography's a roaring fireplace I've pulled my chair close to. I drift off. Memories flare up. The bottle of vodka was full an hour ago. Now it's half-empty. I'm alone but surrounded by men I could easily be mistaken for, it's so dark here. The only light comes from boys' bodies rubbing together way out in the dark. "A fire of unknown origin." Must be the alcohol talking. Time was, and may be again, a guy's body fit neatly into my bed, like a knife fits its slot in the drawer where I organize silverware. I knew love's function, understood its context, put my reaction to it in quotes when it occasionally reared its head. Now I'm holding it under this work like it's something I'm intent upon drowning.

Death is what happens to porn stars these days, especially ones who get fucked a lot. AIDS, the disease that
makes horse sense.

I'm flailing around in the choppy surface of this. I see
Jeff sunning himself on a beach, but he's oblivious. God
won't swoop down, pull me out of this shit. He's a
novelistic device in a remote part of my intellect. My heart
wouldn't recognize Him from the businessmen filling this
row of seats. It falls for obvious things: beauty, distance. I
should be roaming around in this theater like all the other
scum. Jeff's just the subtext of what they appear to be
doing out there in the dark, an unfocused cloud of a thing
hanging over the shoulder of each trick they're jerking off.
I guess the palm of a hand can be Jeff Hunter's ass if you're
hopeful enough. But I'm too tuned to what's what: film as
opposed to life, screen juxtaposed with a room too grim to
light, Jeff beside George, though I tried to confuse them
three paragraphs back.

They're distinct. George is the beauty. Jeff's the statue
erected of him in a public place so he'll remain aloft. We
are the passersby marveling at it. It's the exquisiteness
trying to touch something nearly eclipsed by art. Jeff's just
the shadow that falls across us when we're at certain
points in our lives. By now we know what we've missed
and become depressed. I'm a man brushing tears, imaginary or not, from my face. This is a powerful film, not to
get ostentatious. It's a few men with a few thousand bucks
who are paying a handful of drug addicts to get it up. Jeff
wanders through it like great actors do lesser roles, but, as
far as I know, it's the most significant point in his life.

COVERED WITH DUST, George and I drove in from the
mountains. I kept my eyes on the road. Would he or

would he not spend the night? He took a noisy breath. "Uh, yeah . . . if I can ward off my dad." To look at him you'd think "sweet, pretty, earthy type." But he was a mess, both at that very moment (drugs) and generally. "Unbelievably strange," as he put it. But I'd forget about madness for hours a day, focusing on his lips, crotch, the seat of his pants. Other times I'd sit him down, catch his eye, argue him out of a stoned silence. Slapped him once, which he could barely feel. Held his head while he threw up. Somewhere in there was my lust, an insidious force for good or bad. That's no way to kick off a pornographic account.

If this were pornography it would start something like this: "George was hot . . ." He wasn't. He was sixteen years old with a body some guys would call "boyish" and others would write off. He slid off his T-shirt and corduroy pants, took a shower. Suds encircled his cock and balls. He poked one finger up his ass. He stroked his stiffened cock. "Save it," he thought, remembering his older friend in the next room. Wan smile. What does a kid know from sex? Maybe God could have told me, but He's a myth. "Don't use up the hot water!" I yelled through the locked door. "Yeah, yeah," George sighed to himself.

I stood at the pint-sized pool table my parents had bought me for Xmas. I rolled a series of balls toward the far right pocket. Two went in with a plunk I found sexy at that point. I knew a little bit about you know what. I had wavy brown hair, a slim body, a face friends termed "handsome but long." "My turn," I said as George strolled out, wrapped in a towel. "Yep." He did whatever he did. I washed up. I thought of when he'd agreed to be fucked. "It would be chickenshit not to," I'd argued. George: "I guess." Next stop my folks' house.

Quick call to his mom. Pleasantries with mine. That's
enough buildup.

When I walked out of the bathroom, George was in
bed, on his back, one leg bent, the other straightened
out. I walked over and sat on the bed. "Take off that
towel," he said. I did. I'm not describing what I felt
because I can't. "Struck" is as close as I'll get. Anyway,
I realized if I excised my feelings, that's how I'd seem.
"Moving as if in a dream," as bad novels say. I kissed
George. His mouth tasted like Crest. I caught a crescent
of his lower lip between my teeth. His hard-on throbbed
in my right fist. My left shook his balls like a bag of
marbles. I smeared the tip of one finger with pre-cum,
licked it clean, went back to sucking his mouth. The
lower half of his face shimmered once I'd drawn back.
"Spit in my mouth." He did, clearing his throat first. His
spit was as thick as cum, but much more sweet.
"Again." This time he looked sort of proud as he did it.

In the middle of this is a boy resembling someone else.
Seeing his face slack is what kept my cock hard. It implied much: peace on earth most of all, death next most.
In the middle of what I've just said is a person I feel
detached from. He "gets off" sucking the juices from
some kid he can't see beyond an obsession with physical
makeup. It stands between him and what he desires like
the screen hangs between paying customers and our ideal
lovers. If we charged, ripped it down, we'd find a wall of
unsupported brick. If I'd sliced into George I'd have been
covered with blood, at least. There'd be evidence, if no
answer. But I fastened my mouth to each orifice, stank,
gasped, whatever. I'm looking over my own sweaty
shoulder. All I can see are details (close up) and choreog-
raphy (leaning back). Art, period.

George was extremely attractive. I don't believe I've made that clear, though my cock hardened instantaneously the first time I mentioned his name, if that helps. "It comes down to beauty, doesn't it," I tell myself, not knowing whether to buy that old myth, though I proposed it four paragraphs back as some kind of ultimate. I'm trying to see through that sheen. I've gotten more tangled up than we could have become on my twin bed. The light's brighter now. That just makes the movie itself fainter. George is a jewel in those glittering confines, the same way his heart is a lump of confusing blue tissue two feet up his asshole. But it's not George I see behind Jeff's image, though I'm focusing in on the latter, no more than Jeff would be perfect sex or than sex is what I'm preoccupied with.

I JUST HAD sex in a dark hall behind the screen. I stretched out on a filthy mattress with someone named Ron, Rod, or Rob. I hoped that real sex would set this—I mean me—straight. But I felt farther away than ever from my original hope. I felt a little like God studying something He'd founded only to see a dimension He'd never planned, like a dad probably does with his son at a certain age. I don't know who I expected to fuck, but it wasn't a poorly lit man whose name I couldn't catch. I pulled out my cock, came on his chest. He clenched his asscheeks. Sweat splattered the wall. I opened my mouth. About half of his cum flew in. He licked the rest off my neck. He wrapped his arms around my waist. Nice touch. I felt like saying, "You're sweet," but it didn't suit the occasion. So I said, "Bye, Ro-," muffling the last consonant to be safe.

When I was with Ro- I thought of someone else.
First Jeff reared his jaded head. I grabbed Ro-'s ears,
shoved my cock up his ass until George's face came up
for breath. I fucked him brutally, which is what Ro-
said he likes. I was creating pornography. I tried to
judge how we'd look, where the camera would sit. I
tried to maintain a pace that wouldn't bore people
who weren't directly involved. I wondered if Ro- and I
made compositional sense. I wanted to criticize certain
expressions of his as being melodramatic or, in a couple of cases, too calm for what was actually going on.
When someone's shoving his cock up your ass with little thought for your comfort, you're supposed to look
pained, not half-asleep. A viewer might have thought
we were faking, that I was the one overacting. "Shit,"
I could almost hear some snotty aesthete like me
thinking, "I don't require realism, but . . ."

I had my choice of two fantasies when it was time to
come. One starred two young guys, was a balanced picture. The other featured a guy with a less-than-average
body. One took place in the past, was pristene. The other
was happening in a virtual slum. One was ajar in a
generous way, sharing its wealth with those less fortu-
nate than its director. The other shoved a flabby ass at
your humble narrator for selfish reasons. No choice,
right? I shut my eyes, used the film for a while, then
mutated it. I was sprawled out on a beach in a remote
part of California. Up in the sky a speck grew and grew.
The outline of a boy was discernible. I jerked my cock.
The speck was George. He'd fallen out of a low-flying
airplane, a sexy smirk plastered to his face. He grew
clearer, more fleshed out, the closer he got to earth. I
came as he landed directly on top of me, crushing us both

to death. Now there's a hot porn script. Too bad no one'll ever film it.

The scene onscreen right now is a real piece of shit, featuring a gaggle of has-beens, once-hot boys who've engorged their muscles and added beards thinking that'll appeal to an older set. It feels desperate. I can't distinguish the scrumptious types inside their bulging regalia. They're sort of milling around in an understandably low-lit enclave, taking various oncomers' fists up their asses. It's meant to seem raunchy, but what keeps me glued to my seat is a weird sense of loss. See, one guy suspended in chains in their midst was a porn superstar in 1978, a hustler straight from the Bible Belt playing athletic, college-aged types. Sometimes "Kip" would let some tough guy fuck him, but only if the guy was unbelievably gorgeous. Even then our hero screamed his head off. Now his ass looks like an Edvard Munch painting. Fists glide in and out. "This is the lowest a human can sink" was the catchphrase on the poster outside. I'm supposed to be drawn in by that. I'm touched, but no more than when poring through morning newspapers, past dozens of stricken, anonymous faces. "Kip" was voluptuous. Now he's caved-in like the rest of the human race.

Remember the early seventies? I used to live there. At the time its artists promised a lot, but, looking back, they were just a few refugees from the sixties caving in. Leon Russell, Billy Preston, Badfinger, Jesse Ed Davis . . . names that don't mean anything anymore, no matter how many times revival theaters schedule *The Concert for Bangladesh*. I cared as much about them as I do about Jeff Hunter, more actually, now that I've come. I used to slide down in movie seats with George M., passing joints back and forth. We thought we'd seen God in bellbottoms onscreen wedding the blues and gospel music to country rock. That audience felt united, whether we were or not. But in this dump of a decade these other men and I couldn't be any farther apart, though we're casting our fantasies with the same worn-out, pumped-up ex-teenagers. At best a few guys are jerking each other off out in the dark. I can hear them breathing.

When you're nude you're real. Sounds idiotic, but it's true. That's why porn will outlive art, because it's beautiful in the purest sense. Beauty is timeless. It's the deity panning for gold in these wasted stars' used-up bodies. It creates dreams out of people the cat wouldn't drag in, aiming our cocks at, averting our minds from "the ditch of what each one means," as Bob Dylan whined in the song "Gates of Eden," which is what art is supposed to present us with—routes out of shit holes like this theater. But if this film's an exit sign, then my deity's a mirage, like the image of heaven must be to men kneeling down at an altar. It's just some lost artist's or artists' wild stab in the dark at how life in the clouds would seem. It's scratchy, underlit. But it's the only idea in this theater that hasn't burned out yet, or, like Ro- appears to have done, fled for who-cares-where-else.

(1987)

DEAR SECRET DIARY,

A GUY NAMED Pierre is writing my diary entry for me because I'm too sexually obsessed with him to think about anything else. He asked to write it. He has ideas, big ideas, he tells me. We'll see. When he isn't scribbling he looks into a mirror, for inspiration I guess.

He's about five foot ten or eleven. Tall for a French guy. Great hair, black, curly. Typical skinny guy's back. Bigger arms than you'd think. Pinkish whitish hairless skin. No moles, pimples, scars, weird hairs, tattoos. Typical skinny guy's ass. Bigger legs than you'd think.

My bed is round. It's situated in the exact center of my room and surrounded by stained wood floors. It's the only thing there. It's like West Berlin. When I'm fucking someone and he accidentally falls off the bed, I like to pretend he's about to be shot for trying to defect. Or I did before AIDS ruined death.

* * *

SOMEONE I LOVE as much as I can love died. He was in the hospital wearing a Walkman (it wasn't on) when he just stopped making that horrible sound. I'm inferring this since I couldn't face seeing him. I called once. It was like trying to talk to a squeaky door. You're in a room, reading or watching TV, and there's a draft, and you get so fed up with this door being pushed back and forth that you mutter out loud to yourself, like that would stop the noise. I told someone I knew to tell my friend that he couldn't die, but I don't think the message was passed on. People should live, is the point. Even him. Even like that.

I GUESS IF I had my choice I'd have sex with someone who's unconscious and fairly young. In porn, and sometimes in literature, X can drug his nephew, screw the body, and cause irreparable interior damage, which instills pathos in a contrived scene. In real life, boys scream. When they come down off your drugs, they tell.

WHEN KENNY SOMETHING-or-other was found raped and strangled and dumped, I wrote a satiric monologue in the killer's voice. The death became sexy, disturbing, etc. People laughed when I read it aloud. It gave Kenny permanence, meaning. The real Kenny is bones by now. Hardly anyone knew him. What I believed to be weirdly sexy becomes an occasional thought. (yawn) I'd say more if I knew what was happening to me.

* * *

PIERRE SHUDDERS SLIGHTLY. "That's truly disgusting," he says, still scribbling.

Finally. You about ready?

"For what?" he says vacantly.

(unintelligible)

"Very funny, but what if you give me AIDS?"

(unintelligible)

Pierre looking down at his half-hard cock: "You're scaring me."

Pierre returns to his scribbling. By now he has used up both sides of the page and is beginning to blacken the margins. The paper curls up at its edges like a boat or a large dry leaf. Or a sculpture called *Kenny* . . . Mmm. It's really captured the kid.

KENNY WALKS INTO a bar. "Screwdriver." Since he's eleven years old they won't serve him, but seeing as how he's so cute the bartender says he can stay if he services everyone in the bar. Kenny shrugs and is led to a foul-smelling restroom. He sits down in one of the stalls. The toilet seat is so large he has to splay his legs to keep from toppling into the bowl. All night guys use his mouth for whatever they want. He likes it. It confirms some idea he has of himself. At four they kick him out. He wanders around. A man looks at him funny. Kenny doesn't know what that means, but he sucks the guy off in his car. They get along. Kenny moves into the guy's mansion and lies around by the pool. "I think I could love you," he says, "but it will take time." But after awhile the man gets bored. His friends think he's nuts not to screw

Kenny twenty-four hours a day. "You're welcome to use him," he says, "but I'm telling you, there's nothing there." They do. Kenny starts losing a lot of weight. Some of his fucks think that's hot. They think his sniffling and cough are the result of a coke problem. The "cold" won't go away. Kenny can't get around on his own anymore, so the man's friends pay Kenny's hospital bills. He hates being sick, but he never expected to change the world. He's dying. "No kidding." He's on some kind of machine. No one bothers to visit him, not even me, and I made him up. One night Kenny dies in his sleep. Someone thinks I should know, calls. I listen, thank the caller, hang up the phone, and think, "Big deal."

PIERRE LAYS DOWN his pen, turns around, arches his eyebrows. "That's it? That's the end of the story? But who was the kid, how'd he die, and why?"

You're missing the point, Pierre.

"Which is?"

What's your guess?

(unintelligible)

(unintelligible)

"Look, it's not that I'm not attracted to you, or anything," he mumbles. "It's just . . . it's not that big a concern to me if you want me, you'll have to, uh, force me in some way. Otherwise, I'll . . . *disappoint* you. It's not that I'm not, you know, gay. It's not that I'm scared of AIDS. It's just I don't, you know, have sex that high on my list of . . . whatever. I'd rather talk, or listen to you talk. Or . . . wait. (He reaches behind him and grabs the sculpture called *Kenny*.) Take this. Read it. Print it. *Please*."

*   *   *

(IT'S A DESCRIPTION of Pierre in very hackneyed, glowing
terms, and there's no way I'm going to print it because
it doesn't have anything to do with this diary, as beautiful as Pierre looks today, even upset. But he's my friend,
so I'll tell him he's perfect.)

PERFECTION.

(1989)

SAFE

for Robert Dickerson, Chris Lemmerhirt, Tim Miller

MISSING MEN

Mark had just opened a beer when he noticed an ad in the *Advocate*. It asked for someone like him to write a "beautiful, blond, twenty-eight-year-old lawyer with very specific ideas of lovemaking." He did, with a short but exhaustingly rewritten note: "Dear Tony, if you're the hunk you claim, I'm in the mood for your body. Prove it to me." He clipped a photo booth self-portrait onto the upper right corner. It hid what he felt was his worst feature, shiftiness. The "Mark" he dropped into the mailbox that evening had already gotten "his" shit together.

Four days later he's on the front doorstep kissing his lover when the postman drops a letter in his hand. Mark sees Rob out to his car, rips the flap open. "Dear Sweet Thing, I mentioned specifications. They include your coming by at exactly eleven o'clock Saturday night. The front door will be open. Lock it behind you, strip, and await my instructions." There's a minuscule photograph cut from a proof sheet that Mark has to fish around in the envelope for. He'd need a magnifying glass to be sure, but its subject seems cute. Mark's seen worse.

He spends Saturday morning messing around with his hair, which lies in bangs at the moment, trying to counteract what he's afraid are his face's ill effects: oversized ears, a too turned up nose. Thinking back on the words of a friend of a friend, he makes an appointment with Mothra, a barber famous for steering old rock stars back into the central current. Four hours later, Mark is a new twenty-two-year-old. His black mop's shaved very close to the scalp on the sides and back, the top left a few inches long and tilted forward, sprayed into place at a precipitous angle. It draws attention away from his possible defects. Mark checks himself in the surface of every shop window from there to his Pontiac.

He's attracted to this type, so he should know. He's spent hours on his back longing to sleep with a young man as dolled up as he'll be when he goes out tonight— his face a cleanshaven mask, haircut sculptural atop that pedestal, mascara wresting his dark brown eyes to the appropriate distance, his uniformly gray clothing grounding them, smudging any overtly sexual tone or effect. In theory this look should make him about as alluring as one of the mannequins in these display windows, and it's as hard for Mark to imagine the poseur he's become lying loose-limbed in another's arms as it would be to stand perfectly still in a storefront. But, based on gossip and instinct, he thinks this more aloof, less shy appearance makes him a more attractive person to topple.

His neck and shoulders are stiff the rest of the afternoon. Just the usual nerves. He paces in his one-room apartment, rolling his head side to side, playing the last few records he bought. They share a number of qualities: (1) a rigid, danceable formula, (2) an apolitical, doomed view of life crooned with mock-cheerfulness by the (3) presumably handsome band members staring through low light and makeup on the three covers. Their vocals have a composed, depressed air Mark loves on some level. Its slight chill starts to relax him. He grabs the bottle of vodka, settling down on the carpet. He thumbs through magazines. By ten o'clock he feels suitably, not overwhelmingly calm and struggles up to his feet.

He follows the map west, leaving the tight-knit, condo-packed blocks of his neighborhood for a section of L.A. where trees grow more grand, holding sway over houses; the streets are more winding and wide the nearer the moonlit ocean, the farther apart each antique streetlight, the longer their spreading, respective shadows. This Tony person has money, which doesn't make Mark any less nervous. Despite precautions, sweat inches down both his temples. There goes the haircut. It droops precariously near his damp forehead. He turns left off Sunset Boulevard at Adelaide, making the wheels squeal. "Am I or am I not," he chants as the house numbers ascend on either side. There's the place: Colonial two-story, dark red Porsche in the driveway. Mark aims his foot at the brake but, like a daredevil in his aircraft, veers it up at the last second, pressing the gas to the floor.

He puts on a record and smokes a joint, sitting down on his futon. It and the low coffee table holding his stereo are focal points of his tiny apartment, with a refrigerator, stove, bathroom, and a couple of folding chairs on the sidelines. He has a few posters on the walls. They show pale, smirking rock stars against gloomy backdrops: gutted building, barbed wire, mausoleum wall. Mark rubs his eyes. He's trying not to think about his surroundings. They're a shell of what they might have seemed if he'd traipsed into Tony's and had himself plumbed, i.e., worshiped. That was a fucking palace. This is a dump by comparison, but he would have stumbled home like His Royal Highness if he had guts. He stubs the joint in an ashtray and lights another. The room starts to cloud over.

"RICK HAS RECURRING nightmares in which the ghosts of small boys rouse him out of a sound sleep. They swoop down through the ceiling whooping like braves, dressed in the standard kid garb of the day—shorts, T-shirts, knee socks, tennis shoes—each piece of clothing misty gray. He wakes up startled, seeing the swarm, ducking their balled, see-through fists. First he thinks smoke from a still-lit Marlboro has filled his imagination, then human faces emerge from the clouds. He recognizes some former friends frozen in child state, more and more of them seeping in until his room is fogged with the circling. 'What do you want?' he yells over the din they're creating and, in the process, is awakened."

Thus starts the novel Rob has been struggling over the past year. He is about to shove it in front of his friend Carol, a poet he met last summer in Songwriter's Workshop. He tells her he thinks he knows why it's stalling. First, he's tried too hard to be stylish and clever, thereby gnarling the narrative, except that *is* part of the point, he adds. Or maybe his words are old-fashioned and lavish, "like socialites wearing mink stoles, earrings, hats, and corsages when one item would have been twice as seductive. Anyway, read it." Carol pokes her glasses down to the end of her nose, poring over the handwritten pages. Rob chews his pen's cap, watching a cat outside his kitchen window bat a dead bird back and forth for a few minutes.

Rob's a good catch, in his friends' minds. He's blond, green-eyed, and, though consumed by his writing, socially graceful enough to swing friendships with the illustrious. What feeling's lost in expanding his vision is more than made up for, he hopes, by an ability to see his life as art. Take the case of his new lover Mark, one shot of whom has been framed and is sitting just within Rob's line of sight. In it Mark's camping, lips puckered, eyes crossed. Rob sees a young man who's so comfortable with his own beauty that he can smear it, then see that image displayed without whimpering. Rob chose this picture for the atypical look on Mark's face and because the afternoon it was taken was special for reasons he can no longer remember.

Carol clears her throat. Rob turns his chair around. She says she likes a good deal of the wording, flips pages, stopping somewhere in the middle to read aloud, "There are zillions of clouds and there is twice as much light on the snowfall inside, babying skiers whose hearts are lodged in their throats under cold white mufflers." She lauds the phrasing and continuity of image—clouds lit by ice crystals, mufflers with warm pale skin underneath—but, she adds, there lies the work's problem. Rob has blanketed most of the feeling in what he's describing with his stylization. His prose is a lot like the weather condition he mentions. It's obscuring the subject and blinding his vision. The language needs to be shaken off before it enters the general vocabulary. And in *this* part . . .

Rob bites his lip to keep from rolling his eyes. When Carol pauses for breath he jumps in saying that he *means* the work's mood to be too removed, as overwhelmed by his technical prowess as skiers by the presence of their surroundings. The novel's *about* its embarrassment. If its temperature seems like a problem, then she doesn't see his intentions. Maybe there are some technical miscalculations, which he'd be happy to hear about, or if she simply dislikes the piece and can't admit it . . . He's stopped midsentence as pages of his novel fill the air. They flutter up like doves scared by a child's yell. "Grow up, Rob!" She slams the front door. He sighs, eyeing the disordered papers, and pulls a clean sheet in front of him.

"When Rick thinks back on his younger days, as he frequently does, he sees a vacant lot behind his parents' house, a field he used to spend afternoons in. He best remembers a view from the uppermost limb of an oak tree he almost fell out of once. His thoughts ran wild there. Down below was a dollhouse some unknown girl had abandoned, surrounded by clumps of grass he used to pretend were trees. Once he stole his dad's mower and carved his name in the lot's wild dichondra in big block letters with a short message above it, 'Welcome' or 'Happy Birthday,' as if the whole empty place was the top of a cake decorated in his honor. If so, it's now being thrown in the face of his words as they locate the key to that dreamier time and push the heavy, wooden door of forgetfulness open."

* * *

IT'S MIDNIGHT WHEN Rob suggests they go downtown to
see a porn film. It stars Jeff Hunter, Rob's favorite, a stoic
German boy with a Prince Valiant haircut, lean smooth
limbs, and matching torso. Rob shows Mark the newspaper ad hoping the sight of Jeff pursing his lips will per-
suade him. "He has a dead soul," Mark decides,
scrutinizing it, "but an incredible mouth. Sure, let's go."
Rob puts on soft toast-colored wool pants, a wide black
belt, his ocher shirt, and a thin white cotton jacket
zipped partway up. Mark has on dyed black jeans, black
coat, and a black T-shirt, his typical nonregalia. They
rake their haircuts around in the mirror, Rob looking
over Mark's shoulder.

Rob slides a ten-dollar bill through the greasy slot in
the ticket booth. It's snatched. They're buzzed through
a turnstile. They use the door to the smoking section,
sidestepping potbellied older men who graze the lobby,
slobbering over whatever enters. "Better luck next time,
guys," Rob says. Mark laughs. They walk unsteadily
into the pitch-black theater, taking two seats on the aisle
halfway down. Onscreen Jeff Hunter is in a phone booth
telling some hairy, muscular man he'll be by in an hour.
The guy is shown tilted back in a desk chair in what
seems a less seedy part of town. He strokes his crotch and
drones on about what lies in store for Lord Hunter. To
Rob's slight disappointment it's just the usual "I'm
gonna make dat kid suck my big dick" schtick.

Rob lights a joint, settling deeper into the seat. Mark
is already stretched out, knees hooked over the chair in
front of him, absorbed. He sneaks a half-pint of bourbon
out of his pocket every so often. Their eyes are finally

adjusting. Five or six other guys slowly appear in the rows around them, leering up at Jeff in his tight gas-station uniform. Jeff raps his fist on an office door. The apelike man answers. "Fill 'er up and check the oil and water," he mutters, steering Jeff into his inner sanctum. Rob and Mark snort at the corny, obvious dialogue. Jeff smiles, unzipping his uniform to the navel. "You're Buddy's friend, right?" The ape's jaw drops. The boy's one-piece wafts down to the carpet. "Cat got your tongue, eh?" Jeff continues, stepping out of it. "Or something," the ape manages. He kneels and slips the boy's cock in his mouth. Jeff grits his teeth as it grows hard. His famous ass gets a couple of gentle karate chops up its crack. "Uh," he sighs at that.

Jeff Hunter's face is what Rob likes to call "architecturally sound," but that doesn't mean he believes in God. It simply sounds better than "cute." How many times can you pin a cliché onto someone special? Rob doesn't see the dead soul Mark claimed to, just constitutional boredom, which may be his less-polished term for the same thing. He can't imagine lust crossing Jeff's face, much less fear, regret, sadness, fascination, embarrassment. It seems asleep in its callousness, awaiting a prince with the right-sized appendage who'll pry it open. Rob shuts his eyes, imagining he's a guest star whose cock magically fits in Jeff's locked jaw. They'd drive into the dawn. That sounds ridiculous but no more so than the fantasy he will be living out later, shades drawn and Jeff Hunter "mask" over Mark's unsuspecting head.

Cut to a rumpled bed. Jeff is positioned atop it on hands and knees. The ape's been joined by his buddies. They stand in various poses at bedside, balding and beer-gutted, virtually indistinguishable from one another.

They represent the blinding hunger of millions, Rob theorizes. One slides his head and shoulders under Jeff's chassis to fix the flaccid cock. One checks the oil up Jeff's ass. One does the same in his mouth while the last cleans the upholstery. They surround Jeff as if he is a secret weapon. Rob's fascinated by the director's decision to focus on their exertion rather than Jeff's beauty. "He expects us to associate with their hunger. Jeff's just the bait he's using. Fuck," Rob realizes, "I'm really overthinking this. Must be the marijuana.

"Let's go home," he whispers. Mark makes a faint, agreeable sound. They stuff their hard cocks back into their trousers, stroll outside, jackets zipped over the bulges. Driving back, Rob talks a lot about Jeff's "presence." Mark nods and chews the inside of his cheek. He can't quite see what the fuss is about. The guy was sexy enough, but Rob's moaning like he's seen the Second Coming of Christ, not *Office Equipment* starring Jeff Hunter. Mark is unnerved by how deep Rob's respect sounds to be for that Ken doll with orifices. He also plans to take full advantage of it in a few minutes, bend his legs into a hundred awkward positions if needed. He crosses them and pretends to nod off for the rest of the short spin.

MARK LIES FACEDOWN on Rob's bed, carefully using up half its space. He folds a pillow in half and fits it under one cheek. Rob stands at the foot with a large, yellow towel fastened around his waist. He speaks in a whisper. It carries. His throat has a lump, not from cancer— "Mark," the word that has been on the tip of his tongue all day. It's eroded, enveloped in lots of saliva. Mark peers back over his shoulder. He's heard his name and is trying to figure the tone it was spoken in. Rob's face is darkened, hard to read. He has a hard-on from what Mark can see through thick terry cloth and low room light—a cinematographer's nightmare of moon, all night laundry, and one streetlamp.

Mark is waking up. Dreams burn off. Rob's bed has come into being, one texture at a time. Groggily, between his last snore and initial thought of the day, he realizes he is alone and a sob starts to build in his throat. Three seconds later, blinking his eyes at the usual ceiling, it's vanished. In adolescence, moods that wild were stuffed down inside him, poking out at the most inappropriate moments. He thinks of the day his best friend turned on him and yelled, "Boy kisser!" Kids were squealing, running to classrooms around him. He crumpled onto the cold cement walkway, sure its hard slap was the last feeling he'd have in his stupid, minuscule lifetime.

He's in the kitchen. Rob has gone out for the morning. It's ten-twenty. A note on the table reads, "Lunch together would be possible, if you're interested." "Maybe." Mark plunges into an overstuffed chair in the living room. He lifts the *L.A. Times* from one arm. He scans the front page, finds no one famous has died, and dumps it. He strolls back into the bedroom, squats at bedside, feeding his right arm into the dusty space underneath until he feels the porn magazines Rob's hidden there. He tows out five from the top. One's new. Its cover boy would be perfect without his acne, keeping the frizzy blond mop top, naturally muscular body, and pubescent essence. Mark skims the flimsy narrative past an interminable strip show. Finally the kid works a sweat up, but when he does shove his big cock in a lesser teenager's ass, his countenance grows so blood red, greasy, and mottled that Mark flips the magazine shut with a shiver.

As he does a sheet of paper falls in his lap. The page is blackened with Rob's scribblings but for a space in the upper right corner where he has pasted a newspaper item: RISING STAR FALLS. It tells of a teenager whose stint in porn films was nipped when he fell off a cliff in the lower Sierra Mountains. The article's only a couple of paragraphs long, but the unfortunate's name isn't mentioned until its last sentence. "Jeff Hunter's credits included . . ." The messy text Rob has set alongside this obituary is a fantasy in which he happens upon the boy's body "splayed in the flora and sniffed at by fauna five feet from where he's pitched a tent." With "uncontrollable hunger" Rob mentions finding "religious," he strips the corpse, sucks limp dick, and performs several other activities that Mark's had plenty of after a few phrases.

When Rob unlocks the front door an hour later, Mark's at the kitchen table sipping Jack Daniel's. Rob puts on coffee. "You hungry?" Mark nods. "I found your stash of pornography," he says. "I figured," Rob grins, sitting across from him. "What's the Jeff Hunter thing all about?" Gradually Rob lifts his eyes from his clenched, folded hands. He tries with difficulty to explain himself. He claims it's research for his novel. He says his sentences are like bars on a cage that holds dangerous animals. He quotes a line from mass murderer Ray Sexton's autobiography—"Slapping your partner during the sex act is like changing channels"—equating the shambles that Sexton left high school gymnasts in to the flushed, dripping wet mess Mark becomes in his arms.

Mark sees he'll never receive a straight answer. He tries to look bored to stop Rob's hot air. But Rob leans over, pulling a book by Apollinaire from the long row of thin spines on his knickknack shelf. He turns the pages, locates the poem he likes and points to one particular stanza. "That's how I feel," he says, then sits back chewing his fingernails. Mark reads with a puzzled expression. "See," Rob explains gesturing wildly, "in 1912 critics blasted Apollinaire for making work that promoted disruption. Poems like this counteract those claims by being so beautiful." But to Mark it doesn't clear any cobwebs away, no matter how handsomely it is written.

CARL OPENS MARK'S unlocked door, yells, "Guess what?" and strolls in. John Shane is having an opening downtown tonight at the Kuhlenschmidt Gallery. "Unpack the bags under your eyes," Carl announces, "and slip on something slinky." Mark yawns and sits up in bed. "Who's this Shane guy again?" Carl walks out of the kitchen carrying two vodka tonics. "Well, he's reshaping our notion of static imagery," he explains in the art-magazine jargon Mark finds so irritating. "Carl, turn your head for a second." He takes his usual place at the window, seeming to take in the scenery. Mark throws the blankets off and makes a dash for the bathroom. "I'll tell you when you can look," he says, cringing at what's in the mirror.

In the soft glare of a windowpane Carl can see Mark take a leak, shake his cock, and step into the shower. Through the flawed glass of the stall his body looks like a tiny storm cloud. It edges over Carl's pupils. Carl shuts his lids, thrusts his out-of-shape hips back and forth, simulating the rape of his buddy. "Take it all, lover," he purrs, picturing Mark's ass enlarged and thrown open like off-white curtains. He licks the glass with exaggerated abandon. Mark turns off the running water. Carl grinds his hips to a halt, takes a gulp from his tumbler, and concentrates on the late-afternoon light until his crotch is as smooth as a mannequin's again.

The gallery is crowded. Every trendy, vaguely familiar hipster Mark has ever laid eyes on is swigging wine out of a plastic cup and nodding drowsily. Towering over their heads are twenty black and white silkscreens of naked teenagers. One shows a boy in his late teens slumped on a white wall. His cock is at eye level. His arms are folded over his chest. His eyes are slits, his big mouth gaping in laughter. The word GREAT is painted above his head. "Hmm," Mark says. A second work shows a prettier kid on his back, knees pulled up under his chin, eyes shut tight, as if he's having nightmares. His open ass is the focal point of the picture. The headline NOW DEAD in bold red letters, fills the top of the canvas.

"Oh, yeah," Mark says softly. John Shane's Rob's favorite artist. "A gestural genius" is one of the compliments Mark remembers Rob paying him. Down the same wall a few feet hangs a canvas Mark recognizes from ads in current periodicals. Its youngster has a far harder expression, more bruised-up body, is maybe a hustler. DISAPPEAR is the order accompanying him. Mark feels a hand on his shoulder. "Come meet the artist." Carl's towing him by one elbow into the room's farthest reaches. "Where's my wine?" he asks helplessly. Carl shoves it in his direction.

"Mark, this is John Shane. John, this is Mark Lewis."
Mark shakes the hand of a man in his late thirties, slender and cute in a big-featured way, with expected black clothes and a hip, rockabilly coiffure graying at the temples. Mark lets the man and Carl do the talking. He nods in places whether he hears what they're saying or not, so he won't seem unfamiliar with the art world they're dismantling. Mark could tell Shane was attracted to him when their eyes met. Not only that, he turns to Mark after each pronouncement, eager for some response. "I know," he screeches, "ain't the Gagosian Gallery death on toast?" Mark figures out he's supposed to be laughing. Shane grins, "You know her?" Mark smiles in what he believes is a bored, overconfident way. "So, you're an artist, Mark?"

"No, but my *lover*," he stresses the word, "is a writer." Shane inquires just who this "lover" is. His name's Rob Hall. He's a big fan of yours. In fact, that's him right there." Mark has spotted Rob talking near the front entrance with a few people he doesn't recognize. Shane asks where. Mark points. "Follow my finger." "The one with short blond hair?" "Yes." Shane hides his face from Mark, whispering something to Carl, who answers, "I'm afraid so." Shane turns to Mark again. "You're that one's lover? Or should I say his latest. Listen, hon," Shane curls his lip near Mark's ear, "that young man isn't anyone's lover. He doesn't love. He uses. Typical writer." Mark feels like throwing his wine in this smug queen's face and might have if Shane weren't the fêted guest. That ruckus would be a shade too explosive. "How long have you two been boyfriends?" "Five months," Mark answers. "Well, it should be falling apart right about"—Shane glances down at his watch—"now."

Mark needs a breather. He gulps the rest of his vino, points to his cup, and wanders over to where Mr. Kuhlenschmidt's beautiful lover is serving. "Like my friend?" the oblivious Carl beams at Shane once Mark's out of earshot. "Angelic," he says, "but how'd he end up with that character?" Carl shrugs. "I fucked Rob once," Shane declares. "He's hot. I was half-kidding myself he was sweet for a couple of hours, but the attraction wore off once the fangs underneath sunk in. He can pretend he's Count Punkula luring cute nitwits, but when he's my age he'll realize his aesthetic is merely a curse on him." Shane takes a drag on his cigarette for effect, waits a beat. "Our heads are stakes driven right through our hearts," he smiles, finishing with a fake last gasp.

JOHN SHANE IS veering across the road, shifting his eyes from the broken white lines to headlights in his rearview mirror. No red revolving ones, luckily. Carl is at the controls of the FM, dialing from one current song to another, singing along with those he knows. His dark red hair is uncombed, bangs glued with sweat to the upper two thirds of his forehead, though they've begun to dry and blow free. That's when he's at his best. Shane's not bad-looking, plus Carl thinks a comradeship may be developing with the man, a sympathetic world view or something. If nothing else it'll be worth it to sleep with one of the stars of contemporary art. "Sex is the furnace of creativity; art is the light at the end of the tunnel of words which all life is composed of." Some dead French post-existentialist wrote that. Carl likes to quote it occasionally, obvious though he believes the idea to be.

He loves the paintings Shane's hung in his living

room, gifts from fellow artists, personalized in the corners. "To John, love, So-and-so." He wants to see whose works they are, but when he tries to stand, Shane pulls him back on the couch again. "Wait awhile," he says, drawing out four more thick lines of cocaine on the coffee table. Carl puts a straw to them. "John?" he asks once they've leaned back in the cushions, "I want to ask an important question. Do you live by a system, an organized artistic vision or anything?" "Kid, you're an idiot," Shane cackles, undoing one of Carl's shirt buttons. "I do my best," Carl quips, pretending to be in a mild huff. A tongue zeroes in on his left nipple. It's being pinched. Shane's lips have fastened to Carl's and are swallowing whatever's hanging around in the young man's mouth. Shane's face is crushed against his. It looks as weird as the oil of a drowning man's head, a red and blue canvas on which Carl almost reads the signature, beyond Shane's earlobe.

At times like this Carl starts to wonder what his hero Marcel Duchamp would think, seeing a student of art throw himself into what must be termed a rudimentary act, heavenly though it feels. Sex may be manna, but isn't lust simply a lower life-form relative to aesthetics? Carl's sure Marcel thought so. He imagines the master peeking through Shane's window. Having caught them in the act, Duchamp groans, tsk-tsks, and retreats. Carl's mind drifts from his subject. His hard-on wilts in Shane's mouth like Claes Oldenburg's reputation has in light of post-minimalism. The greatest blow-job on earth couldn't re-create what had seemed massive a moment before. "Don't worry. Mine always goes up and down," Carl whispers. "Just work around it," "Let's go upstairs," is Shane's solution.

Carl is in a room on the second story, staring out of the northeastern window at an expanse of luxurious mansions clothed in the light of dawn. If Fairfield Porter were still alive, lived in Beverly Hills, and worked in stained glass, this might be his masterpiece. The beauty present in nature may be old-fashioned, but Carl admires it nevertheless, though it's no match for a painting in terms of invention. Shane has sneaked up to his guest from behind with a lurid suggestion. Carl shakes his head, but several subsequent hits of cocaine either change his mind or leave him temporarily mindless. He can't tell which. Shane's in the bathroom washing up, pants in a heap at his ankles. Carl's jeans are wadded up on the bedspread, fireplace-warm from his body.

Carl lies on the Chinese rug, grabs his knees, and draws his legs back. Shane kneels before the exposed area. He greases up, feeding a fist into Carl's anus. Its heat is luscious. Carl snorts poppers in an attempt to stay conscious. This is a shit-load of pain, but he'd like to embrace it like a dummy does its ventriloquist, as he senses the hand pushes farther than guts would allow, into his headache, working his mouthful of breathlessness, one finger up the ghost limb of his hard-on, molding that purple embarrassment onto his moderate figure. He wonders what Shane could pick from the inside of his body. He thinks of migrant farm workers, their arms submerged in orange trees across this whole country. He remembers his childhood—one long-gone magician's paw plucking a scarf from thin, colorful air when his fingernails twiddled over a bottomless top hat.

Carl turns his head toward the bay window. Its view is smeared with his sweaty reflection. He gets an idea for a painting, then pain sends it sprawling. He remains still so he can study his abstracted image, as though it were being defused of a powerful weapon. If this were art it would teeter somewhere between neo-expressionist in its obsession with and cooling off of real horror, and folk art, like a statue in the Hollywood Wax Museum. It was posed flat on its ineptly rendered back, while a mannequin in costume as a doctor stood over, gutting the doll of its red vinyl makings. Other statues scattered around had their heads lowered, were even less well constructed but lit somewhat brighter, reflecting more clearly than the tortured soul in their midst or the eye of their "artist," a lack of real feeling in anyone. Or so Carl had claimed in his term paper.

It's daylight when Shane's forearm is withdrawn and rushed out of the room. Shane is scouring it with a washrag and Phisohex. The sun's in Carl's eyes. He's being driven home by the gardener, who keeps his lip buttoned and the car's radio volume down. Lucky for Carl. He's unbelievably hung over. The driver is Mexican and wears dark glasses. They make him seem threatened or vaguely threatening, maybe because he doesn't speak English. What's the difference? *"Gracias,"* Carl says, clambering down from the cab. The pick-up makes a perfect U-turn. Carl pushes open the door to his parents' place. He hits the bedroom, turns on the TV set, finds an old Bette Davis film in which she's going blind, and sits down carefully, staring into it.

BORED WITH THE show he's watching, Rob reads an article in the new *TV Guide* about Robert Blake, former child star of the thirties, now a respected actor, if a "difficult" one. Twice nominated for an Oscar, he's still

coming down from a drug high and alcohol haze that
alienated the critics. They'd elbowed him out of the
business, but he has staggered back in. He is relating a
scene he's just shot for the *Of Mice and Men* mini-series
where he had to strangle another character. To build
sufficient emotion he "searched the realms of my deep-
est self-conscious" and wound up "playing the scene
imagining killing myself as a little kid," a tear-choked
confession that, he insists, proves his newfound, hard-
won maturity. Maybe so, but to Rob it's a usurpable
image.

He yanks some paper in front of him, adding a similar
scene into his novel. His protagonist has a dream in
which he comes upon his younger self doing magic
tricks. The boy bows, pulls a rabbit out of his baseball
cap. Rick's face contorts in annoyance. For complex,
inexplicable reasons, his arms raise into an outstretched
position. He grabs the boy's neck and squeezes. Hunker-
ing over his desk, Rob makes the sweet face crimson. Its
emerald eyes bug out "like the jewels on cheap rings."
Like demons' in ancient storybooks, its features alter,
becoming other lost playmates', hallucinations that just
make Rick more incensed. He rips the kid's cutoffs open.
Rob's knuckles turn white around his pen, against the
darkening hue of that softer skin. The picture he paints
is gaudy, horrid, and somewhat profound, he guesses. If
he were a painter it would wind up on the auction block
for forty thousand dollars.

But it's far more like those light shows at sixties rock
concerts, a few dim home movies projected one on top of
another to no avail, meant to embellish emotions that
aren't showing up on the page. They're not felt in the
first place. Rob is beginning to see that, as his ink slows

to a trickle. He reads the paragraphs he's finished. They
dangle, mere decorations. They remind him of a writer
whose work Gertrude Stein called "a syrup which will
not pour." Rob thinks that quote could apply to the
worst modern novels. Now he's let his own prose grow
so chandelierlike it lights only its own mechanism, not
the life happening under it. He is about to rip the manu-
script into pieces and throw them up in the air when the
phone rings. It's Mark. He's on his way over.

It's nearly dawn. Mark is totally soused. He flattens
out on Rob's bed with a long, ragged breath. He has
been drinking too much lately. Both of them know it,
but Rob doesn't want to confront him yet. That's a
bone that will have to be picked at some later point.
Mark tilts his head up to see what Rob's silence is all
about. Rob gets a sense of how Mark will appear when
he's old and fat. If Rob had met Mark in this more
realistic, unflattering light he might never have coerced
him home in the first place. But that doesn't make
Mark less glamorous now, just more human or something. "You're awfully quiet today, as they say." Rob
shrugs, "The piece I'm writing is shit. I just realized
that." "I just figured out something, too," Mark mumbles, lowering his head. "What." "Nothing."

He has been driving around all evening trying to wipe
out the words someone said to him. That took two
rounds of Jack Daniel's and several joints of Colombian.
He tries to sort things now. He and Carl met at Revolver,
the only bearable bar in West Hollywood. They cruised
the hustler strip along Santa Monica Boulevard, thinking
they'd stop off and earn a few bucks, but were ribbing
each other the whole time. Mark ran into several ac-
quaintances in Second Time Around Records who ac-

companied them to their next stop, the One Way, a
spooky black-leather bar in lower Silverlake. It was half
empty, seemed over. They lolled around in the raunchi-
est corner, praising its heyday, when one drunken kid let
some worse news slip.

Randy is dead: a guitarist on the far edge of Mark's
social scene. He gassed himself in his cold-water flat
Sunday. Mark wouldn't see him for months, then he'd
show up at some party stoned out of his mind. He had a
haunting quality long before he died. "Gentleness" was
the way Rob described it. It shone through wardrobes,
dyed hair, and luded, heavily lidded eyes. They were
light blue and seemed to care where they were, no matter
what trendy bores he was spending his time with. His
friends were anti-romantics with *Billboard* chart figures
for IQ's who'd nicknamed him Crybaby Randy, telling
one another they were in love with him behind his back.
Sometimes he would get wind of it after the whim was
a dead issue. Mark had wound up in the sack with him
once, a year or so ago. Randy couldn't get into it—"too
out of it" in his own words. Mark told their mutual
friends they had fucked until morning, but he'd held the
vomiting boy in his arms a few hours, showered, jerked
off, and hit the light switch.

Mark has fallen asleep. Rob reaches over, drags the
covers to his lover's shoulders. "Good night, you asshole," he chokes, puts his face in his hands. He sobs
until the snoring, blanketed form passes into the back of
his mind, like the storm cloud it resembles. He slams his
fist on the table. He has to get this shit out of his system.
The only way he knows how is to bury it under the
surface of language. He lifts his pen, taps the paper. Ink
is beginning to leak out again. Shortly, with the first

signs of natural light around him, come the first words of a novel so deftly written it escorts Mark, like the lush at an otherwise orderly party, out of Rob's mind. "Forever," he mutters.

MARK MEETS ROB at Hamburger Hamlet in Westwood Village. They stare gloomily at their garden salads all during lunch, eking out the odd phrase or two. "What are you doing later?" "I'm not sure." Rob orders wine, but it doesn't enliven them. Mark just sinks deeper into his own thoughts. Rob's discomfort towers over the meal like the work of a hammy character actor. He chews his nails, taps his fingers on the tabletop, and sighs loudly every so often. "I'm heading home. What about you?" "The same I guess," Mark yawns, stabbing a cherry tomato over and over with his fork. "Well . . ." Rob says, then waits in case Mark suggests something. "Well . . ." he continues, "then . . . I'll see you soon." "Oh, okay." Rob starts to get up, bill in hand. "Are *you* okay?" he asks. Mark nods without looking up. "Call me sometime." Mark nods again, lays down the fork, and they shake on it.

On his way to the parking lot Mark glances into the eyes of a lesbian walking up Gayley Avenue. As they cross paths he realizes it's a boy about fifteen years old. His face is pale, freckled, and clearly Irish. His white jeans and Lacoste shirt reek of having been gifts from wealthy parents, then washed and ironed by a personal servant. He has blue eyes and a red nylon bag over one shoulder that he keeps readjusting. He radiates sexuality he doesn't know what to do with. Mark feels as faint at heart as though the youngster were passing in ghost fashion directly through him rather than just to the left. He slows his step and looks back up the street, but the boy has vanished.

He stops in Le Corbusier for a croissant and coffee. He sips and nibbles. They can't break the spell. The boy was too young to have sex with. They had nothing in common. "Get over it," he tells himself. The kid's long lost. He's sitting shotgun in his dad's Rolls by now, hands crossed behind his head, legs unthinkingly parted, chauffeured through the mock-pearly gate into Bel Air Estates. Mark's in the café's bathroom snorting cocaine in case it's a cerebral Saniflush, but the boy's beauty grows greater each spoonful. He fills his pipe with marijuana to take the edge off. His thoughts haze over. Off in their distance he spies the boy's haunting property—a slight resemblance to Randy. Same height, same full mouth, same scared expression. Mark is reliving the latter's caresses when somebody knocks on the toilet door and yells, "Get your ass in gear!"

He barely gets home. He pulls a beer from the fridge and twists the knob on his phone machine to REWIND, then PLAY. Dial tone, *beep*, dial tone, *beep*, "Hello Sweet Thing, this is Tony of *Advocate* ad fame. You didn't show up at my place last Saturday night, but I'll give you another chance because you look hot as hell. I'll be home tonight, Wednesday. Stop by sometime between ten and eleven under the same conditions as last weekend. Hope to see you then." Mark's first reaction is "Oh no, that asshole again," but in light of lunch with Rob he's reconsidering. He takes the pipe from his jacket pocket. After three hits he looks into the bathroom mirror. He sees someone who's cute though wearing out, good for a complimentary drink in a packed bar, maybe, but hardly fit for the archaeological dig Tony's probably planning.

He tries on every tight-fitting pair of jeans in his mea-
ger collection. He combs his hair straight back, to either
side, down the middle. He's back to square one: his
naked body. He turns, bends over, and peers through his
knees at the butt upside down in his mirror. It's his chief
asset. If he can only find clothes that direct all attention
to it, even slacks with giant arrows all over them. God
knows his ass pays back all eye contact in spades—
creamy white, small and firm, almost no hair in the
crack. To him it may be a cushion, but he can see why
it's so mouth-watering to certain cognoscenti. One of
humanity's great mysteries is how much of an icon the
rear end has been, for gays in particular. Spreading its
cheeks very wide with his forefingers, Mark thinks his
own even slightly resembles the Shroud of Turin. But
he's begun to feel dizzy in this position.

"Fuck it, I'm going out." He puts on jeans, a T-shirt,
and stumbles off to the stereo, digging out his favorite
record. Its doom and fashion sense waft from the speak-
ers, through the lead singer's stiff upper lip. Mark sways
around in its breezes: "Gods will be Gods / but when
mine opened up / I was made out of skin / and bones will
be bones / but when I came home / there was no one
in." He mouths the lyrics. There's a draft in their thinking that chills him each time he listens. He wishes he
could have sex with the sullen young man who intones
them, but he is farther from that British star than his
heart is from the music he's lifting this diamond needle
from.

MY MARK

Mark stands in the windy darkness outside a nightclub. He teeters, bracing one hand on the wall at his side. He slurs a few swear words, pressing the other hand to his head, which is covered with sweat. He wipes it off on the front of his T-shirt and leaves his palm there, feeling the rise and fall of his chest, the word *Maxell*, his heart. One of his knees gives out, but he catches himself on a drain pipe.

The coke he's snorted and scotch he's been swigging all night make it seem unimportant. Mark wants to wander back into the club, but he's sure he is going to puke. In a matter of seconds, in fact. The front door swings open. A few strangers shove their way past. He bends suddenly at the waist, throws up, getting some on the wall before he can lunge to the left and heave the rest in some bushes.

He drops to the pavement, rests his elbows on his knees, and puts his face in his hands. It's a decent one. Its decency lies in its lack of incentive, the blank kind of face that one finds on the inbred boys of the South, those backwoods he'd hitchhiked from. Looking at it, one couldn't glean his intention, the mood he is in. "I couldn't say," Mark's face would mutter if it could speak for itself, like the moon's almost might, if it wasn't so cold and decrepit.

Color is back in his face. His breath is quieting down. A few pedestrians stop, seeing he's ill. When they're sure that he'll live, they rush off. Mark glances around. No one's looking at him, but the scenery's getting in focus: a run-down hot spot, several patrons, their nondescript clothes. Their faces are low-burning lanterns that stoned bodies carry. Such faces show off the ideas inside with an undermined light, at least to his taste.

A man meandering by decides that Mark's hot. Mark notices this. A place to sleep and some money: his second, third thoughts. He gazes back, hoping that sweat hasn't given him up. Said man walks over, crouching in front of him. They stare at each other up close. The man isn't much, has a hard-on, looks gay. "Can you walk?" Mark doesn't know. It's a good question.

"Try." Mark puts his hand on the man's back in order to keep his balance. He feels drunk but hardly spectacular, wobbly in other words. The man caresses Mark's ribs, spinal cord. He fans out over the hip bones. They're broad and sculptural, barely padded by flesh. And in the boy's face the man sees the skull that is propping it. Mark's eyes roll back in his head. He pulls away, falls down, and, holding on to a bumper, vomits into the street. The man waits until he is finished, then hoists him back up.

Mark really stinks now. He's sure about that. He's glad this guy's indiscriminate. He hasn't stopped groping Mark all the way to the door. Mark's bones, actually. A duplex. It's dark inside. Mark trips on the rug but catches himself on an end table, brings it crashing with him to the ground. A lamp just misses his head and shatters against a wall. He has to piss, but the man has already toppled on him. His T-shirt is over his head. His jeans are folding up like accordions at his feet. His ass may as well be a new best-seller, the way the man thumbs to its dirty part.

Mark's on his knees and one cheek is against the carpet. The man puts his head by Mark's ear, muttering less than a stream of consciousness, more than a string of clichés. Mark reeks of sweat, vomit, and what he's been drinking. He wants to piss, sleep, and that's about it. *It* is the best that could happen right now. The man settles back on his haunches. Mark's ass hunches up in the air, courtesy of its skeleton, which the man has envisioned inside.

The man grapples forward and locates a skull in Mark's haircut. He picks out the rims of caves for his eyeballs and ears. The lantern jaw fastens below them, studded with teeth. He comes to the long shapely bones of Mark's shoulders, toying with them until two blades resembling manta rays swim the surface. He clutches his way to both elbows. Ribs ride short breaths to the touch. He grasps Mark's hips, and their structure floats up to him. He strokes through a reef of wild femurs that keep up the ass. He lowers, hand over hand, down each thigh bone, past knees, negotiating sharp ankles, and finishes off with an inventory of feet.

Mark hears the man come. Okay, so that's over. He raises up and glances over his shoulder. The skeleton turns to stare at its lover. Whatever it's thinking, it always looks like it's laughing at the expense of a boy who's in sparkling focus. The man's eyes are spooked when they look at him. The man grabs and kisses the apparatus on its lips. Then he lowers his bony companion to the floor. It just lies there. The sound of a shower goes on in another room.

Mark combs his hair in a mirror. The man comes out dripping, puts on a robe, and starts straightening up. Mark asks for money. The man shakes his head. The boy's face blurs as he does. Then it clears, but he still sees the skeleton there. It's a premonition. Its glee is the truth behind Mark's bored expression. Mark puts his hands in his pockets. A light through the open door silhouettes him in his last few seconds. He lowers his eyes. "Bye."

MARK GOES ALONE to the top of the hill and stretches out on his back, looking into the sky where an endless succession of darkening clouds drift over, shadowing him for a second or two at a time. Sure, it feels peaceful, but after a few minutes that shit gets boring. He stands up, brushes the dust off, and heads back down.

At the foot of the hill is his parents' new condo. He puts on the brakes, slowing down to a jog as he reaches its steps, and strolls up. Nobody's home. There's a drawer in his mom's bedside table that is as low to the ground as a doll's, with two tiny knobs that Mark's fingers can barely keep hold of when sliding it open. It's longer inside than you'd think, and his dad's .45's hidden there.

His mom has a floor-length mirror. He stands a few feet from it, holding the skinnier end of the cold blue-black barrel crosswise under his nose as a mustache. His father shoots antelope in the eye, then ties them onto the car trunk. "Heil Hitler," Mark says in a soft Southern accent.

Mark's face is supple, secured to his bones in slight ways, and thin-skinned, so he reddens or pales with different expressions. Guys think he's handsome and talk up his flesh tones. But as an older friend told him, "Anyone's cute at your age," although Mark looked around and saw that was shit. His friend's just attracted to "youth."

Mark's dad was once a hapless farm boy in Georgia. Mark was a crazy idea in his head—one more squabbling, lightly flushed blob indistinguishable from the rest of his first-grade class. Mark sat in back by the windows because it was farthest from anyone, though he was told they would shatter and snow in his eyes when the bombs hit. He'd be found centuries later, crouched under beams that had beaned him, surrounding his head with stars.

This room is lit poorly, designed to look just like its twin in their old house, where Mark had been born. Bulldozers crushed the original last Wednesday. That hurt, but it fell without anyone trying to save it, while Mark stood around on the sidewalk eyeing the hard hats and fussing with what he was wearing.

He met the eyes of one worker, filled his own with something bordering on longing, and managed a few similar words of encouragement. "Hi there," for instance. He and the fellow met up in a bar late that evening. Sometime the next morning Mark let his jeans be unbuttoned. It took thirty seconds. He watched his face in the skylight. He'll never forget how impressive he looked as long as he lives.

He lives for moments like this, being totally calm in his own way, seeing himself in a mirror, or the more distant reflection of him in the face of a man who is trying to give him an orgasm he doesn't want in the first place. Mark puts the gun to his head but would never pull the trigger. He likes the people he sleeps with but hasn't gone overboard. He's bored when he thinks about anything else but sex.

MARK LEANED BACK on the wall, his black curly hair closely shorn. Last year it was long. He still seemed angelic, a bit more mature, though his eyes hadn't lost their inviting look. *I* felt like I was on something, but had a hard-on; the best of both worlds. Mark's words were all slurred.

He wore a tweed coat that somebody who'd rimmed him had bought. "Nothing romantic," he said. I signed my name in his copy of my book. I scribbled his number on half of a sheet of loose paper. I wrote his name in my tiny black booklet where poems start out lines of words dreamed up when coming on people like him. We shook hands. Now it's weeks later.

Mark's on his hands and knees in Marina Del Rey being rimmed by some man who is paying his way around town at the moment. He's stoned on excellent acid. His cock isn't hard, but once was. His ass is pink from a few light slaps, more on the way. He's ten stories up in a high-rise. A window looks over the ocean.

The man has his face in Mark's ass. It smells like a typical one, but belongs to a boy who's a knockout, so it's symbolic. It's sort of like planting a flag where no human has been. Well, maybe a few old explorers. It's sort of like putting on makeup in front of a small fogged-up mirror. It's an expression of caring.

The seat of Mark's pants is draped over a TV set, undies kicked under the bed in the hope he'll forget about them. It's the end of their day, the beginning of mine. He'd just be spreading his ass with his hands and fitting it over my face about now, if he were smart and didn't need money, would settle for gold in the eyes of a guy who is gaga for him.

The man screws his eyes up. Mark's anus is wrinkled, pink, and simplistically rendered, but nice. All that licking has plastered its hairs to their homeland, smooth as

a snow-covered countryside seen from a distance at sunset. Closer, the ass has pores much like anywhere else,
only more refined.

On TV some cowboy is shouting, *"Arriba!"* It sounds
like "I need you" to Mark, and he smirks for a second.
It sounds like "amoebas" to the man rimming. He's
risking them, so he can find out what makes this boy
happy. He leans back and takes a flash picture. By the
time it's developed, the sight of this asshole will sicken
him.

Mark falls asleep and the man has his face in a washrag, in soap that smells heavenly after that last place.
Mark has crashed out on his stomach, the usual pout on
his lips, his ass crack reflecting moonlight. It looks like
a blaze in a faraway valley. "Not far enough," thinks the
man in the bathroom. He dresses and goes for a walk on
the small man-made beach near the harbor.

He looks up at the window. It's low lit. I like how it
is now. It makes me seem less like a ghoul where I am,
dreaming of someone I barely know. Mark sleeps his way
through the rest of this story, face down, like someone
who just shot himself in the temple. Spray flies on the
man who is thinking things out. Has Mark been worth it?
What did he want from the boy in the first place?

He wanted the same ass I do, their eyes met, and they
danced to a Gloria Gaynor number. Mark saw the cut of
the older man's clothes and thought, "Money." The
man saw the ass in Mark's corduroy pants, connected
it up to his Caravaggio face, and thought, "Bull's-eye."
He hadn't pictured the odor, which he got used to, then
paid for.

One evening Mark shared a joint with me in the men's
restroom. I came back smacking my lips like a demon,

friends tell me, which is the story that led me to make this concoction, which I'd like to blow up in Mark's perfect face like a poorly planned chemistry project. I wish it was like in the movies, where this would backfire and I'd end up wiping my eyes, face black with soot. Wish I could be there.

The man walks out onto the jetty, all the way to its end. From there his building looks less functional and prettier. The boy in his slumbers, stretched somewhere therein, is as small as a doll that the man couldn't play with. He'd feel too embarrassed. Mark's long white body is warm where it is. The man shivers thinking of it. It's a godsend, granted, that's leading him back to the shore again.

The black ocean rolls on forever. A boy being tucked in, that's easy to figure. Mark's ass is a moon to the moon. One dripping-wet man stands around in its low light, putting it out with a sheet, blanket, coverlet. He goes to the window and looks at the jetty whose top seems too small to have walked on. But he knows an illusion when seeing one.

I see myself in the man's position, though more on a level with Mark in the sense that I'm brighter and less prone to unbridled worship. I'd ask Mark to stop if he yelled at me. I don't have the money to pay for him. But here I am blocking the view of this simple scene, like a director who accidentally walks in front of his own projector, then stands there, oblivious to the snoring around him.

A pretty boy and a wealthy man sleep together. Their body types can't be made out from the heavy bed clothing. The lamp's off, which buries them deeper, then my eyes adjust and I find them. Man on the left, boy on the right. No sign of struggle, except in my voice as I try not to care for them, feelings I've slipped from this body of work like a boy steals a richer man's wallet.

What's left behind is Mark's beauty, safe, in a sense, from the blatant front lighting of my true emotion, though it creeps in. I'm moving stealthily closer, I think, to the heart of the matter, where Mark's body acts as a guide to what he has been feeling. That's his, like great art is the century's it was created in, though still alive in the words of a man who speaks well of him. "Mark keeps me going."

MARK WAS ON drugs a friend said, so he must have been really beautiful. He lived by the ocean two hours south of here, with Preston Adams, a rich older man who was trying to start an affair with him. Mark said, "No way, man," then came back to earth minutes later, a little bit wealthier, to shake his friend's hand and start undressing.

When Mark was older and thought I was someone important, he used to motorbike over, listen to records with me, go get Mexican food, smoke a joint, stand around with his hands in his pockets, look at my books, say how stupid love was, then ask if I loved him. I guess at the time it was sexy. Now it's just more of what gets to me.

These thoughts are more about me than my friend because when I was with him his looks left me speechless. That kind of beauty is insular, fills all my words anyway. What I construct must divide him from them in slight ways, such as placing the warmth of his skin against clinical language, like flesh of a man who lies down on a sharp bed of nails and is saved from real pain by the evenness of the impression.

Mark held his liquor. I'd get undressed in the bathroom. He'd be in bed with the covers up to his nipples. His hands and his feet would be cold until I warmed their details. He'd lie there fumbling for words in a shy way. We'd talk, and when one particular sentence ended his mouth would stay open. We'd french. I'd slobber down to his cock, making several stops on the way, bend his legs back and fuck him. He'd do something similar to me, and etc.

If you need to know what Mark looks like, see the gay porno film *Give Me a Hard Time*. There's a guy in it named Sandy, a box boy who's picked up hitchhiking by sailors and raped in a ship's hold, then disappears from the movie. He's skinny, dark-haired, very pale, smooth, and about five foot seven. He's listed in the credits as Steve Getsuoff, and in close-ups, his eyes are too serious.

I have a note that Mark scribbled when he got up in the morning several years ago. It isn't much, but it came at a time when his body was near me, so I unfolded it hopefully. It said, "Dear Dennis, I wish I could stay but I couldn't. I took a peach and borrowed a book. Don't go to see *Love and Death* and I'll see it with you tomorrow. I'll call from the bus stop." Part of it's faded, then . . . "your Mark."

That's just one semiarticulate fragment of what's still important. I found it deep in my file cabinet under "Mementos," along with a few other stragglers. It's strange how something tossed off could have been so impressive, like the graffiti that piles up on neighborhood walls, which I stopped looking at after a few months, but which I've heard has been raised to the level of Art by the experts, simply because it's expressive of one human being.

One morning I took Mark's face in my hands, having unfastened the front of his outfit, once we'd begun kissing. I hoped to see why I'd read so much into it that summer. His skin was cool and expressionless. His eyes looked warm but were clearly kidding, and with all that distance between us, he may as well have been gazing into my camera lens like he did several weeks later, standing in his doorway. That photo's propped up in front of me this evening.

A HEAD THAT has power over me. A globe lightly covered by pale flesh, curly black hair, and small, dark eyes whose intensity's too deeply meant to describe or remember the color of, seemingly smeared and spiraling.

I fill a head with what I need to believe about it. It's a mirage created by beauty built flush to a quasi-emotion that I'm reading in at the moment of impact: its eyes on mine, mine glancing off for a second, then burrowing in.

Its face is pale and unmemorable. My eyes give off fear or indecision. Its face is lit from below. My fear is lit by my face. It's scary but warming, like some long-lost pumpkin set on a darkened sill. It had two poorly made, gentle, and endlessly flickering eyes that would scare me when I was innocent, although I'd carved them myself.

It couches itself in expressions that value a force past its flesh, fit very tightly to delicate bones whose eyes reflect what they intend in illusory ways, with some sort of murky belief held so many levels below that they can't be described for the beauty of what's keeping it.

My eyes are warm in the middle of this. They hold my

body out, which I offer free of restraints: these flimsy
blue nothings I'm wearing. But its eyes are cold, have
been out in the open too long, got carried away. What's
left is ice where love lay such long hours when younger,
covers the idea of something under their forgotten color,
like the representation of life that a prisoner leaves in his
bunk at a jailbreak, seemingly sleeping away.

It eyes the reward of a power greater than loving, that
stormy opinion that simply erupts in smudged irises,
leaving this holiest look in its path. I want to slap it. It
wants to soften my blow with the more heady vision of
what lies below: its hairless body, the sense of which
can't slip past well-tailored clothes meant to color a head
that has some wits about it.

It rests on its hand, and it stares into space like the
head of a dying boy, vaguely aware of somebody he loved
or despised in his lifetime, but hollowed out now with a
whittler's patience, which leaves these black slits for its
eyes and the sign of some thinking around them: a mask
that's been saved for all year, then shoved on the skull
of a friend, to affect me.

I'M HERE ALONE. Mark is in Washington, D.C. Craig is in
Downey. Julian's in Paris. Robert, David, and Shaun are
at work. They were my lovers. Now they sound more
like the names you hear paged in an airport and sort of
wonder about. All of the fingers on my hands extended
mean "presto change-o," which, aimed at somebody important, can't make him love you but, used on Mark's
shoulders, seemed to relax him a little.

There's an odor inside the body I can't figure out,
unlike a crotch's, and worse than the ass's reminder of

brunch, snack, or dinner. I've read about it in novels: the madman poised over an innocent victim, his knife at the end of its trudge down the teenager's chest, which, like the earth in some scared Californians' opinions, splits open upon the least provocation. The murderer, thinking of rummaging inside the torso, is driven back by a frightening stink that writers leave in obscurity, stumped as to how to describe it, not having smelled it.

Without it Mark's not complete, but it lies slightly out of my grasp like the big ring of keys to the door of the jail cell where somebody somewhere is probably locked up for strangling some kid he couldn't get love from. He'll reach as far as he can through the bars and never get near it. I mean the truth about anyone.

Mark's still a mystery to me. He was, in part, a young man who happened to wind up with well-balanced features, knew what to do with his eyes, and I exaggerated his power, as it was a time in my life when I needed to feel very strongly. Mark filled the bill. Seeing his face on first meeting, I was so speechless that friends had to turn me around and shake my shoulders.

When I was younger and met a boy who I wanted to sleep with, I was too embarrassed to say so. I'd lie there wishing that he was in trouble or dying, so that my feelings about him were justified, then I could say it to him on his deathbed—*it* being "I'll always love you"—and he would die thinking of me. Now I'm too embarrassed to think of the people I care about dead, and those who I love may as well be starring in their lives around me, and I one of tons of admirers breezing by.

Once Mark took me to a magic show. I was called onstage to assist the magician. I was amazed by how phony his sparkling tubes looked. He pulled something out of my ear. I felt stupid, was famous for weeks in a vague way. We saw a man with a partially paralyzed face who did some pretty good card tricks, but all the magic was ruined by having to watch him perform. Later we heard he had died.

I miss Mark. I aimed my feelings right at him. He moved back to Georgia, left no address or phone number, and was "lying nude in the dark listening to music" the last time I heard from him. I loved him. I should have said so less often. It got so his eyes wouldn't register that kind of input. He'd lie there thinking of something or somebody so far away that he seemed dead, and I'd have to rub his skin like a frostbite victim's until he knew I was home. That's an exaggeration.

This is a time when independence seems important. I keep my guard up. I've got a dim trace of wit where my heart would be turned up full volume and pointed at someone. I have less sex with more people. I should just say things are okay, I guess, like I would if questioned by cops about it. Once they impressed me, but so did the bullies who hit me with math books and left me prone on the ground. My father found me asleep at my train set and carried me up to my bed.

"Wake up," Mark yelled at me. "Look around you. Get your fucking life into gear." My life was great and that wasn't what he was trying to say. He'd walk around in the evening slamming doors rather than say what he meant, which was what I had asked for. I was probably drunk, hoping I'd die or he'd stop me, one or the other. I couldn't speak my mind either, so I emptied a fifth of tequila into it.

I have a photograph of Mark and me against a white wall that could be anywhere in the world. We look in-

credibly happy, having been drunk on our asses seconds
before. We have our arms around each other's shoulders.
I'm more ecstatic than Mark, and he's more determined
to look great on paper. It was a luminous moment. My
line to friends upon showing it is "We'd have made some
great babies together." Their eyes roll upward.

"In blindness that touches perfection a hearse is like
anything else." Ian Curtis wrote that. He sang with a
rock band called Joy Division. Hearing him sing such
things in his deep, quavering voice, I had the sense that
he couldn't get close to his feelings, and his embarrassed
attempts were the subject of what he was doing. He
killed himself before getting respect for that.

"I knew this would happen. I remember the first day
I met him. He said, 'Hi, my name's Ritchie White. I'm
on probation.' " I stole that line from a movie because
what the young boy pronouncing it really wanted to say
was "I liked him." He felt too stunned to. The fellow
named had been shot by police when he pulled out an
unloaded pistol. Ritchie was brown-haired, brown-eyed,
smooth-skinned, and bored, then he rotted away in the
ground. His friends set fire to their school to feel better.

I'm trying to get to the truth, just like they were, so
that even when looking into the eyes of somebody who
doesn't care about me any longer, or never did, I'll be
strong. Mark used to make me seem helpless. Back then
I wrote in my journal, "When I'm with him I feel perfectly calm and when I'm not I want to jump off a
building so he'll never stop thinking of me." Now I've
added in a steadier hand, "I couldn't have meant that."

Certain things mean a great deal to me. Mark did. My
father does. Sex does. Being a friend to a great person
does. So does the knowledge that I'm alone, although

praised to the hilt by some people, even when loved so intently I don't have to think about concepts like love any longer, which I've never been, nor would have realized if I was, which doesn't matter, or has been hopelessly screwed up by me and won't come back.

Once I held high hopes. I'd loved Mark, found that emotion was possible. He was a small human shape climbing into a car at the end of the driveway. I knew that he'd become much less important to me, but there I was writing a letter, so he'd at least understand things a little. He called me up when he got it. We talked for hours, and when there was nothing but awkward silence left, he said, "Then let this be it, okay? Promise me." I promise.

BAD THOUGHTS

There's an incredible softness about Georgia. It's in the air, which, no matter the weather, feels as tenable as mist on your forearms. It's in the messy green fields rolled up against each horizon and in manicured lawns you imagine the dead could draw back like a comforter if they tried. When Doug was there it was sweltering. He stood with Mark's family, former lovers, and childhood friends, about whom he'd heard a few stray comments. Doug saw Mark's looks in his mother's, though it is possible he mistook her somberness for Mark's boredom with him toward the end. There the comparison ended, as she began to gasp. Sobs were induced around Doug. People slumped, lurched forward, choked, and moaned in chorus. In Doug's shock it felt like bad drama. He couldn't conjure up anything close to tears and stooped self-consciously, wincing at his sneakers.

When Doug was younger his parents would slap each other and wind up crying in separate bedrooms. It was the only time he remembers them showing emotion. Once it burst so fiercely out of their scrunched hands and faces he wanted to leave home. He got as far as the basement. Thunder subsided as they discovered his note, read it aloud, phoned his friends who knew nothing, then went out and clawed through the bushes. Finding they cared at that distance made him feel better than when they'd sit down on his bunk bed, trying to say so. These days Doug can't voice his own feelings, though he's sure they would sound wild as an ocean if he could put his ear up to the boy's skull where he whispered them. It's in a plot outside Athens, Georgia. Doug's going there in his mind, thinking Mark's resting place, like that musty basement, might drag him out of the state he's in.

He'd just plugged the key in his rented car when one of Mark's other lovers leaned in the window, suggesting a beer in the nearby gay tavern. Parting the fog bank of cigarette smoke, they set their Lights on the end of the bar and eyed some gathering youngsters, mostly hustlers at that hour. Greg had met Mark here in late 1979. They fucked around for three months, then settled into a townhouse. That lasted two. "Beautiful boys are the craziest," he sneered, pulling his hair back to show Doug the scar left by one of Mark's beer bottles. "Like Dwight down there," and Greg tilted his head toward a silhouette near the pool table. Through the dark Doug saw a tattered lampshade of a teen in huge T-shirt and loose jeans.

"We could take him to my place for twenty-five dollars," Greg elbowed Doug. Doug nodded. Greg was a stranger, but Doug felt unusually close to this fellow survivor of that "disaster in blue jeans," as Doug's friends called Mark half-affectionately. Doug downed his beer. Greg stuck his arm in the air and waved the watchful tramp over. Next thing Doug knew Dwight was limping ahead of them into a sunken living room, laughing at everything they were saying. Doug accidentally ripped Dwight's blue T-shirt. Dwight bit his lip, bending over the back of the sofa. There's an incredible softness about even wrecks of boys when they're so pliable, Doug could imagine Greg and he were pulling taffy instead of ironing out stretch marks. Dwight drawled a few rules and moaned professionally. His back was smooth. When Doug shut his eyes, the bruises blended right into it. "Jesus, I'm coming." They paid the youngster. Doug dropped him off at the Eagle and found a motel room. Cher was on Johnny Carson. Doug flew home the next morning. He doesn't want to think about them any longer.

Sometimes Doug wishes that whole period of his life could fit into an old-fashioned shadow box like those he'd turned to the light at his grandparents'. "Before the photograph, there was a better way of holding beautiful memories," Gramps used to tell Doug, "if you were rich enough to afford it." He could look into a peephole and be right back there in 1902, Grosse Pointe, Michigan. It was a simple illusion accomplished with levels of painted paper. First the low cast-iron fence in the foreground. Then a green hillside of yellowed gravestones. Then the second, more densely packed hill. Then a bare mountain with a white cross on top. Then the blue tissue paper. Presto. If Doug were good with his hands he would build a box with those ingredients and a red X to mark Mark's tiny grave. He'd press his toy to the windowpane, sob a few times, slip it back in the dresser drawer, and meet his friends' eyes again.

IT'S BEEN FIVE months since Doug thought about Mark every day. He's fading, gradually, like a song Doug used to love on the radio, once kids stopped calling up to request it. Doug used to work the mouth of a telephone like an evangelist with a cheap microphone, yelling thousands of miles in the distance at Mark: "Come back." Mark's tinny voice, with its disregard for Doug's hysteria, might as well have been "God's" it rang so inhuman. Doug was possessed by the abstractness he'd invested it with, as it changed from a tropical whisper into the kind of anonymous speech of an intercom calling D students to the principal's office, except Mark's was telling Doug to give up. He only did at the news Mark had died, the details lost in a relative's sobs and late-night long-distance static. He put down the receiver and stared into space, until light from the following morning swept his ceiling.

He spent the next few months in deafening dance clubs under blinking, revolving lights, gravitating toward baby faces with a spooky resemblance to Mark. He was drunk. They shone across rooms. He'd stop in after eleven, make his way to the bar, order a couple of what fucked him over, and stand on his tiptoes to look around. Last summer one's eyes met his, so he stumbled over. They dished the crowd, ditched the joint once its overhead lights came on. They had a beer on the roof of Doug's building. Todd said, "Great view," pointing up.

His bangs fell into his eyes once he'd fallen asleep.
That's Doug's idea of perfection when drunk. He lay
gazing up at the plaster as contentedly as if a skylight
had been enthroned in it for the evening.

When Doug was Todd's age, ten years ago, some
friends and he used to drug themselves out in his parents' house, feeling one another up under the sprinkling
of fluorescent stars Doug had painted on one ceiling.
They thought they understood love because he'd been
able to re-create one tiny fraction of its atmosphere in his
bedroom, but their ménage had as much to do with real
love as poster paint with heaven. Doug put on spacy
music. They drew straws. The loser let everyone else
shove a finger up his ass. Doug rigged it. When his turn
came he studied Larry's asscrack as if it were an open
atlas. Larry looked over his shoulder. The near align-
ment of that boy's dim butt and pale face eclipsed Doug's
nervousness, though he pretended to barf as he drew out
his digit. Later Larry and he tiptoed past sleeping buddies
and kissed frantically on the balcony.

Todd was standing on Doug's balcony when Doug
woke up. He seemed in deep contemplation of predawn
hours, but when Doug joined him he said he was thinking of jumping off. Doug rubbed his eyes and looked into
Todd's. They contained mysteries great as those he'd
glimpsed through now rusty telescopes. Todd was wearing Doug's blue robe. Doug was torn. Todd's eyes teared
up as he described the hollowness of his existence.
Words echoed between the buildings in his flat timbre.
Doug said, "But . . ." several times. Todd cut him off.
No hope, no love, no peace, no drugs, no time. This was
the gist of Todd's moaning. Afterward he seemed to calm
down a little.

"Sorry," he said sheepishly, dressed and left. Doug

watched Todd's ass disappear out the door. Its smell still
rings in Doug's mind if he concentrates. He knows he's
being obsessive, but that's his pattern, one thread con-
necting the dots in his scattered life, a solar system of
smirks and tight assholes he glued his lips to with no idea
who he was looking up. Todd still calls sometimes when
he's out. They meet for drinks, see a band. He's formed
a kind of attachment to Doug, though sex is out of the
question. "Why?" Doug asks every so often. Todd
shrugs and changes the subject, though once they took
LSD at the Griffith Planetarium and kissed like lovers,
imposing sexier features on faces they barely made out in
the dark. Doug imagined Mark briefly. He was covered
with chills, but it was only Todd's skin in the air-condi-
tioning.

   Doug and Todd are birds of a feather. That's why
they're friends, two sad sacks filling each other's head
with thoughts of death until one of them flies off the
handle or picks up somebody else. With Todd, Doug says
what he wishes he had to Mark, trying to make amends.
Early this morning they strolled on Santa Monica Pier,
counting constellations. When it felt right, Doug told
Todd he sympathized with a death wish aesthetically,
knew Todd would never actually kill himself, but
whether Todd did or not he'd like to say farewell now,
as a dumb kind of formality. Todd was so drunk he said,
"What the fuck!" Doug threw his arms around him.
Todd mumbled, "See you pal." It was over in half an
hour. When Todd pulled back it was daylight. Doug's
trying to focus his eyes in it.

DOUG HAS A passion for pornography. It's both a world he
can think very clearly about and the purely aesthetic

experience he feels most comfortable with. He has a row
of magazines twelve inches long on his closet shelf. He's
dipping into them this afternoon. He's been collecting
since high school, when they had titles like *Lust-In* and
featured overweight long-hairs waddling out of bellbottoms. Gay tastes were less refined then, but Doug main-
tains the affection for those prototypes one does for one's
first lovers. Ten years back he longed to writhe like an
epileptic at the tips of their flicking black and white
tongues. Now the guys he was so rabid for might just as
well be silent film stars, they're so outdistanced.
They've become representatives of what Doug perceives
as a sweeter, easier time, waving from fuzzy photographs
like presidential candidates from the backs of trains.

Thumbing through them toward the glamorous prep-
pies in recent releases, he takes his time, experiencing
the relaxation of being alone, as well as the slight edge
an actual roll in the sack would throw into him. He dusts
off *Peace of Ass* from the sixties, pulls *Disco Balls* from
the mid-seventies. *Punk Spunk* from later that decade,
and the spanking new *Gym Sucks.* He flips past hippies,
androgynes, clones, punkettes, and settles down on the
couch with two handsome young jocks making moves on
a wimp in a dorm-room set. This wimp's the reason
Doug laid out $12.50. He's Jamie Wingo, whose sly face
and ass have been Doug's favorites for a decade, from
Wingo's first small role as a kid "raped" by "political
activists" in a "crash pad" in "San Francisco" to this—
his juiciest part yet.

He plays "a stranger" the two hunky "lovers" have
lured on the pretense of good marijuana. To Doug it's
they who are strangers, and this perspective engenders
both a wariness of their motives and fear for Jamie's

DENNIS COOPER

safety that just makes his cock harder. The jocks don't
care about Jamie like he does. They prop him up, lay him
out, turn him over, eating and pounding his orifices.
Blond fucks his ass and Brunet plows his face until Jamie
folds like an accordion, at which the "lovers" lean over,
french-kissing each other. It is as though at this moment
Jamie doesn't exist and they're alone together. That's a
perception that chills Doug and, when he comes seconds
later, he is relieved by its sense of well-being.

The life pornography pictures is ordered: inhabitants
may treat each other like pieces of furniture, but when
the last page turns over they're usually back in their
jeans again, none the worse for the wear. Doug wants to
live in this one-dimensional world, have hot sex twenty-
four hours a day, leave one bed, fall immediately into
another. If someone he fucked died he'd never hear
about it, and if he did the word wouldn't compute or feel
real to him. He'd be involved in his latest orgasm, face
drawn so tight nothing else could get under. But dreams
won't buy him a hustler, much less his ideal lover, so he
gets up and takes a long shower.

IT'S TWO-TWELVE A.M. Doug's awakened by Todd's phone
call, ordering him to Undo, the hottest after-hours club
in West Hollywood. There's a band Todd's heard a lot
about headlining there tonight and "we should check
them out." Doug had been planning to sleep off depres-
sion, but Todd's raised, wobbly voice is a clear distress
signal. He's fucked up. Doug relents, staggers up to the
basin, splashes cold water in his face. The club is a
former Mexican restaurant, La Siesta. Doug "can't miss
it." He finds Todd waiting around near the garish en-

trance, leaning against one green column, cigarette plugged in his lips. "Take a deep breath," Doug says. Todd manages to walk steadily past the club's bouncers.

The place is packed with hip gay men in black outfits, plus a few youngsters who've dieted down to their skeletons and draped themselves with dramatic silk tunics in bright, misguided attempts to re-create a better century. Doug eyeballs four kids with foot-high blue mohawks, hunched over Pac Man machines. They look familiar. Sure enough, when lights dim they climb onstage. Two hang guitars over their shoulders. One sits at drums. The best-looking rests a thin arm on the mike stand until their fans calm down. "We're Horror Hospital," he yawns. "This song's called 'Psychotherapy,' which me and Devan"—he flicks his head at the bass player—"are going through, if you know what I mean."

Doug tunes in to what follows. It sounds like shit until a kind of chorus pokes through. Then it's attractive. People around him have started to roughhouse, i.e., "slam dance" in the current vernacular. Doug and Todd take a few steps back, clearing a fire break between them and the jostling. Doug recognizes the wildest dancers. They're friends of Todd's who redo their looks every few months. These buzz cuts, pallors, and shades must be about on the way out. Their flailing used to bug Doug, particularly at parties. Now he's met several and found an attractive naiveté in their voices, as misplaced as a ventriloquist's behind the wooden expressions.

Deep in the brawl, tossed around by a slew of boys twice his size, is a pasty-skinned teen who'd make Doug's eyes extend five feet out of his face if life were a comic book. His dyed black hair's in a blustery heap atop his head. His fake bohemian wardrobe is carefully

messed, from the tip of his cowlick to scuffs on his boots.
Doug bets he lives in Bel Air, has a Mercedes-Benz and
A-plus average at the top private school he's a big outcast
at. In high school Doug fell in love with thin, gangly kids
like him, bright boys who slunk along edges of gym
classes making bad jokes about muscular, pea-brained
classmates. Doug used to stand around, drooling at what
was so underdeveloped on them. Now these same scare-
crows are chic and, like those lucky guys in the sixties
who had gargantuan Mick Jagger lips, sleep with the gods
of their generation for the moment.

This boy reminds Doug of somebody he used to sit
around with by the gym wall while most of his friends
were huffing and puffing on ball fields or clouding parked
cars with dope smoke. His name was Lon, and his haircut, though merely uncombed, shared a halo effect with
this punker's more carefully misrendered mop top. Lon
talked a lot about lounging around his bedroom listening
to records. Doug threw out hints for an invitation. Lon
never asked. Doug used to picture them a half-inch deep
in some shag rug gone quicksand while rock 'n' roll
records blasted above them, saluting what they were
doing, which if Doug had had his druthers, would have
found his index finger up Lon's ass. It's practically all he
described in his journal that year.

Semesters later, when Lon had gone off to college,
never to promise to call again, Doug read an article in a
now long-defunct underground newspaper about a Hollywood stripper club where women danced on a long, pier-
like runway. The girls would squat and spread their
vaginas inches from customers' eyes. Each man would
scan his assigned one, handing its towering owner a
ten-dollar bill. The article centered on a man who, when

a stripper knelt over him, pulled a small flashlight out of
his pocket to gaze up inside her wild organ. The woman
spread it especially wide and was paid particularly well.
"This guy just had to have *pussy*," the journalist wrote,
putting the word in italics to mean he'd wanted the
Truth. That need makes sense to Doug. He's imagining the punk onstage right now, nestled back on his
haunches directly overhead. Doug would train his pen
light on that enlargement and learn its deep secret.

Doug is snapped out of his fantasy by hot breath on his
left ear. It's Todd. He's seen who Doug's mad for, thinks
the kid's hustling, would be happy to try to arrange
something if Doug likes. When Todd's stoned, he feels
invincible. Doug's used to humoring that phony Super-
man, but he's so wowed by the boy that instead of his
usual sarcasm he nods. In a few minutes Todd's heading
back, hustler in tow. "You two get acquainted," Todd
says. "I'll see you later." He winks and makes for the
bar. Doug sticks his hand out. "I'm Doug Landau." The
kid shakes it. "My name's Skip . . ." he says, wrinkling
his forehead in concentration, "Skip Skull."

SKIP STUMBLES LIKE boys his age do in exploitation
films—axes lodged in their backs—but he's just drunk.
Doug helps him down the hall, shuts the bathroom door.
He hears him gagging in there. Doug picks red lint off his
T-shirt and closes the curtains, hiding each sharp instru-
ment within arm's length of the mattress. Skip walks
into Doug's bedroom chewing his fingernails. "I used
your mouthwash," he mutters, then strikes a half-assed,
bow-legged attention. "Skip Skull reporting, sir. What
are your orders?" "Hit the latrine again, private," Doug

smiles. "Shower and douche a few times. Then get back here on the double." "Figured," Skip sneers. "Bullshit," Doug thinks to himself.

Skip makes a point of parading his rear around, joking about its "needs." That's not as sexy as he thinks, but when he sits next to Doug at least his belt's loosened. This is the hard part, to get Mr. "Skull" in bed before the boy's cover's blown by the dumb sense of humor, flamboyant anecdotes (". . . had by the biggest and best"), and other sundry shit barreling out of him. He's a real blabbermouth. Doug knows his favorite bands, siblings' names, parents' occupations, and is beginning to care. If he doesn't move soon his game plan of bouncing Skip off the ceiling will be the informal, friendlier show of affection he's less adept at.

"You about ready?" he blurts. Skip nods, stands, removes his jacket. Doug hits the lights and unzips. Skip stands beside him, nude, radiating light heat, wondering what to do. Doug drags his last shred off. Skip grows impatient and sits on the bed, swallowing yawns. They distort the lower half of his face unbecomingly. Quick, Doug thinks. "Lie belly down." Skip complies, peeking over his shoulder at his own ass with renewed confidence. It has a permanent flex like a marble statue's. His Tenaxed haircut makes audible cracking sounds as his head hits the pillow. "Shit." "You okay?" Doug whispers. "Yeah," Skip says. Doug pulls the cool buns apart, looking down at a fresh, unmarked asshole "God" probably thought would be safe in such a remote place. It suggests good genes and years of light usage. Its taste reflects what Doug can't put his finger on because Skip thinks that might "stretch me out," as he whined earlier.

When Doug was Skip's age he saw a photograph of a boy pushing his face in another boy's butt. For reasons he thinks he'll never know, it held power the beaver shots, fondling, and cock-sucking couldn't. He'd started targeting asses anyway, and kept a scrapbook with photos of famous ones: Michael Parks's in *The Bible*, Leonard Whiting's in *Romeo and Juliet*, John Phillip Law's in *The Sergeant*. But Doug wouldn't have known what to do with one if he'd been handed it on a TV tray, besides cradling it in his arms, a chaste kiss on each cheek. One picture answered Doug's burning question with bells on. He stood dumbstruck in the back row of Tom Cat Adult Books staring down at a genuine masterpiece. He stuck it under his coat and strolled out. Over the years this singular act has become the big theme in his swelling collection, and in his lovemaking. When gasping bed partners wonder why, he puts his tongue in his cheek to tell a true story.

"Once there was a man who founded a town in New England. He was a homosexual, gambling, drunken old lout, so the family buried him quietly in a nondescript graveyard beside other rabble and bums of the period. Over the years tales were wrongly told and records misplaced. He was forgotten. One day, eighty years later, committees were formed to reinstate him on his proper pedestal. Money was raised and a monument planned into which his remains would be slipped like a battery. But when they dug him up they discovered a root from the neighbor's apple tree, one whose fruit was renowned for its sweet flavor, had pushed through the man's coffin and devoured his body. Townsfolk were eating the flesh of their forefather each time they bit in those crisp, red apples." Skip's reaction is typical. He looks perplexed and lies flat again.

The pinkish skin of Skip's buttocks erases everything but its essence for more than an hour, each metaphor, image, and symbol of death haunting Doug's head. What's left is a few pointed thoughts. "I can't lick deeply enough" is the main one. Doug pulls Skip's buns even farther apart, sprucing the crease up. The anus mouths the words "Thank you," with help from Doug's probing thumbs. Its pucker raises the hackles on his neck and grows so loose he could slide in his cock without raising Skip's eyebrow. He prefers a simple tête-à-tush. He sees the art in it. He sculpts until his eyes glaze over. "I've got to crash," Doug says, raising up on his elbows. "Come if you're going to."

Skip lifts his hips and jerks off. Doug is too tired to. He yawns, telling himself not to give the poor kid a good-bye kiss. Money changes hands. "Sure I can't drive you home?" "I'll take a cab," Skip says, dressing. "I'd like to," Doug mumbles. He thinks the long stretch of freeway between their neighborhoods would do the work of black coffee, waking him from what he wishes were sound sleep. He feels obligated, tired as he is of this youngster. They stand in the front doorway. "Umm . . ." Doug says, pausing to reconstruct what he'd intended to say. ". . . well . . ." he trails off again. Tired too, but out of a sense of politeness, Skip starts to thank Doug for his hospitality, sees the bored look on his face, and walks out the door with a shrug. "Whatever."

DOUG HAS A porno magazine in his left hand. He's stretched on his back, closing his eyes. An image stays in his mind. In it two handsome young men are french-kissing, their tongues so tangled one can't be picked from the other. Doug likes to think the slightly less glamorous model is shoving the cutie's aside in his hunger for beauty. That makes more sense to Doug than a commingling, and in his own version he's tickling Skip's tonsils. He milks kissing for what it's worth, laps the neck, cleans an armpit, and slurps his way down to what he remembers of Skip's feet, which isn't much. "Skip" lies perfectly still, breathing inaudibly. He is conveniently rolled on his front when Doug's ready to zoom in. Soon as his tongue is in its "musty holster," as Mark used to call it, Doug comes, hurling his head around.

"Skip" stands, throws on clothing, and leaves. Doug opens his eyes. He thinks how stupid he'd look if the real Skip could see the mess he's made of his life. No chance of that. Skip's just another pair of used asscheeks Doug will kick like a beach ball into the sea of former ideas. Skip's washing out on a series of cursory thought waves. "Bye Skip," Doug says to himself. He lays the magazine on his bedside table, next to the clock. Eight-twenty A.M. Now that cum's out of his system he'll get some work accomplished. His room's a dump for one thing. He turns the radio to a New Wave station. He zigzags wall to wall, putting clothes, LP's, and books in their places. Under his dresser he finds the towel that Skip smeared cum on the other night. Doug presses it to his face. It smells like every other pretty guy's dried sperm except Mark's, which, though cut from the same cloth, had a distinctive air. Or maybe Doug simply imagines it more rare-jewel—like in retrospect. That's it.

"Mark," Doug whispers. His name keeps coming up. Doug shakes his head roughly side to side like hippies do old acoustic guitars in which they've lost their picks. It seems to clear out. In fifteen minutes the room sparkles more or less. He's wondering whether to use his remaining strength on the kitchen when the phone rings. "Hi Doug." It's Todd, who's "just checking up on my handiwork," which means Doug's roll in the hay with "the kid" last weekend. "Godhead," Doug declares. "I had him facedown, butt-up for eons. It was incredible." "Say 'Thank you,'" Todd says. "Thank you." Silence. Doug senses Todd's slight annoyance. "He said his name was Skip Skull," Doug continues, "and he had the ass of death. I'll never brush my teeth again." "I think you're making a mountain out of a molehill," Todd answers. "What's this crap," Doug thinks, but says instead, "Just different drums, I guess." Silence again. "So what else do you want to know?" Doug goes on, humor plummeting out of his voice. "Just that," Todd says. "Fine, well then, see you." Doug hangs up.

It's dark out. Todd's at the front door, yelling, "Doug!" Doug lets him pound a few times and walk off. He's not in the mood to dig Skip up again. He *is* in the mood to disinter someone however. But porn will have to do. He grabs the magazine off its perch. It's *Swap Meat*, which he originally bought because one of the stars seemed a burlier, tattooed Mark Lewis. In the months after Mark's death, *Swap Meat* grew tattered in Doug's attempt to move into it. He squints while turning the pages, as if attempting to view a great work of art from the proper perspective. It doesn't hold up. Even an image he'd thought religious this morning is just a snap of some junkie on hands and knees, beckoning over one shoulder, eyes drugged to pitch-black, asshole fucked so many times it resembles an empty eye socket. Here's his drab tassel of penis and balls dangling down one bruised leg. "Yuck!" Doug shuts the magazine.

He closes his eyes, concentrating as hard as he can. He

can't quite tune the real Mark in. He gets a familiar face, but, though evocative, it could be Mark's, Todd's, Skip's, the porn star's, or others who've caught Doug's eye in Mark's wake. Features have piled up, superimposed until the visage Doug sees has the beauty but blankness of a *GQ* model's. Mark's is somewhere beneath it, a skull whose gleaming originality can't be touched no matter how wildly Doug imagines he's french-kissing. Mark is a pile of bones deep and unlit in the earth. Doug's lost in thought. His cock's hard; his brow is furrowed, but he might as well try to breathe life back into someone who's been dead for so long he'd be totally brain damaged. "Face it," Doug says through clenched teeth. He reaches over, lifts the phone, and dials a long-distance number. But when a snowy voice answers, he hesitates for a second, then hangs up.

DOUG IS WALKING along the beach, or what's left of the beach after last night's storm. His Ray-Bans cut glare in half. The sand is littered with chunks of painted wood, parts of the pier two miles up. It appears totaled from here, Doug thinks, kicking a small piece three feet. Boys in their teens are searching for souvenirs they can cart off on their bikes. One youngster carries the leg of a carousel horse like a club. His eyes look scared, steel-colored, and, Doug guesses, full of dry wit. He's older than most of the others. He acts like a cruel camp counselor, shooing small boys from the real treasures. Their ten-speeds, parked in a perfect, tilting row on the ruptured sidewalk, have the absurd names of Hard Rock bands felt-tipped all over their spans. "Quiet Riot" is one Doug thinks he's heard of. He pulls a six-pack of beer from his tote bag, lowering down to the sand.

The boy whose reflection is centered in each lens of Doug's glasses wears loose trunks with a suggestive rip up the ass. His ribs are showing. His inch-wide nipples jut out like a young girl's and probably cause him trouble in certain quarters. A boy at Doug's high school was teased about his "tits" until he withdrew from classes. He and Doug used to hang out and free associate about "Get Smart," making up episodes full of wild sex. Lusting for the near-impossible is a great hobby of Doug's, be they actors in now unwatchably unfunny TV shows or this pale boy bending over a bunch of junk. He has a long, sleepy face and blond hair that could use a cut. Doug's watching so intently the boy notices. Doug lifts his beer to say, "Want one?" not sure if it's the right tack. But better a chat with some boring kid than the word "faggot" chasing him up the beach.

"Like one?" Doug asks as the boy approaches. "Sure," he says, dropping his club. His voice is high-pitched for his height. "But," the kid adds, kneeling next to Doug, "we'd better keep it cool. If my friends see me drinking, they'll all want one." He grins and Doug sees his eyes aren't so spooked, just dilated. He's on some drug, most likely. He turns his back to the boys he knows, lifting the beer in a neat arc to his mouth, upper arms clamped to his sides. He glances over his shoulder and, sure his friends are preoccupied, gives a low whistle. "Greedy guys," he mutters. Doug's basking in the boy's warmth when Truth dawns on him. It's Skip: sans Tenax, black rinse, and mascara he looks completely different, far plainer, his eyes less sunken. "So, Mr. Skull . . ." Doug begins to say. The boy cuts him off. "Skip Atkins, actually," he declares, and his sunburn grows shades rosier. "Sorry about that," he adds. "I get in weird moods sometimes."

Skip's bike is clanging around in Doug's trunk. "Tell me where to turn," Doug says. Skip is slumped down in his seat, singing an endless song about cars that's beginning to grate on Doug, great as it may sound in Skip's head. Skip pretends not to hear what Doug's said. He's already announced he expects to be "kidnapped," as he put it half a mile back. He pokes white spots in his burned skin. It looks like satin in this light. Yesterday Doug thought he'd used Skip up. Somehow the boy at his side is untouched, more a volunteer who'd dodged swords in a magician's locked box than someone Doug ate out. He's still in perfect shape. "Why not?" Doug thinks. He turns at the next light, heading for home. Skip quits howling and places one hand on Doug's shoulder, pointing out White Stallion Liquor Mart with the other.

They sprawl on Doug's bed, drinking shots of rum chased by cold Bud. Doug's tipsy. Skip seems soused. He's talking a blue streak about things he barely knows, like the band that played Undo on "the ill-fated night," as Doug calls it. "They're just the best," Skip slurs, but when Doug asks for one reason Skip blurts, "Because they're cute," then shakes with laughter. "*Dry* wit?" Doug chuckles, reflecting back on his earlier impression. Fuck aesthetics, he thinks, not that they mean that much. If they did, he would have left Skip back at the beach. He's nowhere close to Doug's type. This is the first time in over a year he's been with someone who looks so little like Mark. With a big swig of rum, Doug tells Skip he's an unusual case. "I mean it," he insists. "That's great," Skip smiles, patting Doug's leg.

Doug and Skip have rolled off the bed onto the rug. Skip lies facedown with one leg of the overstuffed chair in each hand as if braced for a violent wind. He's said "Shit" so many times the last half of it's worn off. His ass and Doug's balls meet up with a light slapping sound. Their breathing only embellishes it. They're in different worlds, but with each slap realize they're not alone, no matter how far away their dream boys may ride bikes or lie dead. Doug knows whom he wishes were here. He wonders who Skip is fantasizing about. He whispers, "Skip," to see what happens. "Skip," the boy's voice echoes back. Later he laughs when Doug tells him about it. He can't remember what he was thinking. "About being in pain, probably," he sneers, then adds, "Just kidding," in case Doug's easily hurt. They watch TV in bed. Cartoons at Skip's insistence. Doug gets tired, turns on his side, and is shaken awake an hour later. "I've got to go," Skip announces, back in his trunks. "I like this book," he adds, holding up *Naked Lunch*.

Skip climbs on his bike. The paperback's tucked in a safe place. The merry-go-round chunk is strapped to one thigh with an old rope. Skip's off to visit a friend who lives nearby. "I'll call you," he promises as the Schwinn click click clicks down the drive. "You better," Doug shouts with mock-insistence. "Watch out or Skip Skull will," the boy yells, pedaling out of view. Doug snorts and walks back in. He cleans his bedroom. Next to the bed is a Polaroid he shot of Skip. It's blurred because of the way Skip spun his head when Doug called to him. "Shit." He drops it into his dresser drawer, on ones of

Todd, Dwight, Mark, Lon, Larry, and others, going way back. He's had a pretty full life, he decides, glancing over the pile, but not so full that the drawer can't be closed tight.

(1984)

EPILOGUE

for David Salle

T HIS PIECE IS haunted like an old house. It sat two blocks from my parents' place, bike-riding distance. The sun rose in the sky like the flaw in my fingernail arcs toward the day I will bite it off. This piece limps toward the world with one part missing, and in its place, the phantom pain of a boy's stance in my life.

Its central figurine can't get his due. Joe got bored, flew out the front door, is referential material built from the scraps he left lying around. For instance, I have a faded tuxedo ad we posed for. It was the late sixties. We were supposed to be "hippies" glaring suspiciously at "bourgeoisie" in our midst.

A blue light suffused the sky. The grass was painted green. The world is faked, head to toe. That's my dad's necktie restraining my long hair. I smirked when I was

159

told to pass judgment on lives that dwarfed ours for the moment. "God" is the adjective I like to use when describing Joe, as it implies beliefs lost in the years since.

This piece has more in common with a tuxedo's luxurious order than our conspiratorial glance. Shyness invented our faces. Fear culls the words I write. Joe's beauty veiled the real world. Our lack of savoir-faire ruined that ad. This world appreciates its faker aspects. Back then no one believed in us.

The ad was a monument to itself. We were just chipped, toppled statues, compliments to a gray suit that civilization raised to a concept we'd written off. We were extremely pretentious to think we could represent more than our drugged selves. I like to praise things that don't deserve it.

No matter how I position it, that time's a threat. It stirs in its throne room of phony light like a young boy who's constructed a dollhouse around himself. If I could finish it, I'd hide behind all this artifice and stab him hundreds of times, which is what I've been doing here, but I'd replace this blue pen with a knife, this page with juicier flesh.

The photographers left. It was just Joe and me and the afternoon. We would have lasted five minutes stretched out like that. Boredom, I mean. "Haunted house," I thought, motioning toward our bikes. Ten minutes later we snuck through its rusty and vine-draped gate.

Its crisp front yard was a mess, the mansion shaggy with flakes of preweatherproof paint, from its peaked roof to the lopsided front porch. I pushed open what was left of the door. Joe trailed me in. His back, ass, and legs became part of the inner dark. I'd picture them and lose my train of thought.

Maybe if Joe were here the whole issue of art would seem pointless beside him. I close my eyes and imagine he's lying facedown. My hard-on enters his ass; my knife repeatedly stabs his back. His life is upped in its preciousness. I can continue to work.

We climbed the dangerous stairs, checking each room. Someone had scrawled FUCK THE PIGS in toy blood on one wall. Joe wore his TIMOTHY LEARY FOR PRESIDENT T-shirt. Blue letters, white cloth. His mood turned ugly at one point. He threw a can of dry paint through a pane of glass for kicks.

What did Joe want out of life? Something that only a head dull of drugs could suggest. Stringy brown hair, pinpricks for eyes, but I lusted after him no matter how many days in a row he had worn those pants. It's him I loved, not the idea of love, nor the effect of the joints we smoked, nor the descriptive abilities I've picked up since.

We crouched in what used to be someone's room. Remove the concept of ghosts, bulldoze the sketchy set, eliminate gothic overtones, and what's left: two seeming nobodies fumbling for things to say. "Let's try the roof." "If you're sure we won't fall off."

I was Joe's beau, big brother, dad figure. That house is our love distilled into one spooky scene, where truth and wishes commingle. His sense of me was a little of both. My sense of him is complete fabrication. How could I know what went on in his head? Not by watching the back of his pants precede me up those steps.

The roof was falling apart. Loose shingles broke off and clacked to the ground as we strode across. It seemed the perfect spot to stretch out, light up. I wanted to fuck him right there and then. The danger implicit in our surroundings made compositional sense. I saw the big picture before I knew what was under my nose and behind Joe's illustrious face.

He was obscured by the smoke from a flickering joint. Instead of Joe, I saw a yellowing ad for the boy I'd have held if I wasn't so stoned out. He and the smoke and the skyline of trees seemed unnaturally poised, so my eyes took a photograph. Ours was a vague, high-gloss world with unsuitable tension inside it.

I can remember when, many years subsequent, traveling in Europe turned into a chore: flus piling up, tiffs with my traveling companions. I walked by myself to the tip of a jetty in Nice and stared out at the Mediterranean. Its turquoise depths were incredibly turbulent. I was "at peace" for the first time in decades.

Looking in Joe's eyes felt like that, the actual turbulence "lost" in their overall blueness. I thought, "Just go ahead and fall right into them. He's stoned and won't know the difference." We kissed for a while, then drew slightly apart, watching my hard-on deflate. I felt like tossing him down on the roof.

He felt (1) peace, (2) afraid that refusing me would test our friendship, (3) guilty, (4) disappointment at what he perceived as my hidden intentions, (5) used, (6) drugged, (7) ?

Now, even more than then, I want to know. Once I imagined an autopsy in which Joe's feelings were pried open, figured out, placed in a poetic light. They're in a short story I'll never publish. But love's not like that. It eludes words, which are all I know how to create. It throws an old can of paint through a thin, polished work of art, then dashes off.

I rest my hand on my chest. Joe is still in here somewhere throwing things around. He grabs a handful of words and breaks the hearts of those trying to get a good look at him. I say his name in a low, dispirited voice to no one in particular. I sound like a foreigner, don't I, man?

Joe is alive in the work of an artist obsessed with him, trapped in a cave-in somewhere in these long-winded sentences. I could abandon him, then live my life with a tiny, prickly voice in my head. Nothing a few drugs won't tone down. Or I can push all that's left of its door open and throw some light on that rickety house, or whatever remains of it.

All that remains is this cold black rectangle of words I've been picking at. My eyes are peeled, but I can't see a thing for the dimness of what felt more bone-chilling back when I scaled its heights. Now I will lift my blue pen off this darkened page and check its structure for highlights, with chin in hand. A haunted piece in place of the love I would dream of from here on in.

(1985)

Acknowledgment is made to the following publications, in which these stories appeared:

"A Herd" and "Dinner" previously appeared in the book *The Tenderness of the Wolves* (The Crossing Press, Freedom, CA, 1981); "Container" appeared in the catalog of the Tony Greene painting retrospective *Exhausted Autumn* (LACE, Los Angeles, 1991), and in the magazines *ZZYZZYVA* (San Francisco) and *Chemical Imbalance* (New York); some of "Introducing Horror Hospital" appeared in the magazines *JD's* (Toronto) and *SHINY International* (New York) and in the chapbooks *He Cried* (Black Star Series, San Francisco, 1984) and *The Missing Men* (Am Here Books/Immediate Editions, Santa Barbara, 1981); "Wrong" appeared in the magazines *Between C & D* (New York), *Homologie* (Amsterdam), *Thing* (Chicago), and *L.A.I.C.A. Journal* (Los Angeles) and in the anthology *High Risk* (New American Library, New York, 1991); a piece of "Square One" appeared in the magazine *Soup* (San Francisco), and the entirety in the anthology *Harbinger* (Los Angeles Festival / Beyond Baroque, Los Angeles, 1990); "Dear Secret Diary" appeared in the catalog of the multimedia exhibition *Against Nature* (LACE, Los Angeles, 1989); some of "Safe" appeared in the chapbook *My Mark* (Sherwood Press, Los Angeles, 1983) and in the anthology *The Faber Book of Gay Short Fiction* (Faber & Faber, Boston and London, 1991), and the entirety appeared in the book *Safe* (The Seahorse Press, New York, 1984); "Epilogue" appeared in the magazine *Bomb* (New York), and in the anthology *Dit Verval: Een Grote Ziekte met en Kleine Naam* (De Woelrat, Amsterdam, 1988).

165

ABOUT THE AUTHOR

DENNIS COOPER IS the author of two novels, *Frisk* and *Closer*, and several volumes of poetry, notably *Idols* and *The Tenderness of the Wolves*. With choreographer Ishmael Houston-Jones he has created seven dance-theater works, most recently *The Undead*, which premiered at the Los Angeles International Festival in 1990 and subsequently toured the United States. He has written on contemporary culture for *Artforum*, the *Village Voice*, *Interview*, *Art in America*, the *LA Weekly*, *High Performance*, and elsewhere. Widely anthologized, he is also the editor of the anthology of rebellious lesbian/gay fiction *Discontents*. *Jerk*, a book created in collaboration with artist Nayland Blake, will be published in May 1992 by Artspace Books. Born in Pasadena, California, he has lived in New York City and Amsterdam and now lives in Los Angeles.